"You Make A Breathtaking Princess," Jacob Said.

"Don't say that."

"Why not?"

Allison's glance snapped up defiantly to meet his. "You wanted me to marry you for a purpose, to clear the way for your future. I'm still just a small-town librarian who's playing a role in a little melodrama you and your advisers have cooked up."

"You're far more than that."

He had to remind himself that he couldn't tell her everything—not now, not until he'd worked out every complex detail.

In a way, he realized he was being selfish again—but this time he felt no guilt. He was determined to get what he wanted, and he was willing to risk everything—his father's approval, his countrymen's love, Allison's treasured independence...perhaps even more.

Dear Reader,

Happy Holidays to all of you from the staff of Silhouette Desire! Our celebration of Desire's fifteenth anniversary continues, and to kick off this holiday season, we have a wonderful new book from Dixie Browning called *Look What the Stork Brought*. Dixie, who is truly a Desire star, has written over sixty titles for Silhouette.

Next up, *The Surprise Christmas Bride* by Maureen Child. If you like stories chock-full of love and laughter, this is the book for you. And Anne Eames continues her MONTANA MALONES miniseries with *The Best Little Joeville Christmas*.

The month is completed with more Christmas treats: *A Husband in Her Stocking* by Christine Pacheco; *I Married a Prince* by Kathryn Jensen and *Santa Cowboy* by Barbara McMahon.

I hope you all enjoy your holidays, and hope that Silhouette Desire will add to the warmth of the season. So enjoy the very best in romance from Desire!

Melissa Senate

Senior Editor

Please address questions and book requests to:
Silhouette Reader Service
U.S.: 3010 Walden Ave., P.O. Box 1325, Buffalo, NY 14269
Canadian: P.O. Box 609, Fort Erie, Ont. L2A 5X3

KATHRYN JENSEN
I MARRIED A PRINCE

SILHOUETTE *Desire*

Published by Silhouette Books

America's Publisher of Contemporary Romance

To Lucia Macro and Cristine Grace, my editors, who
love prince stories as much as I do...and gave me a
chance to tell this one. My deepest thanks for your wise
guidance and priceless suggestions.

 SILHOUETTE BOOKS

ISBN 0-373-76115-5

I MARRIED A PRINCE

Printed in U.S.A.

KATHRYN JENSEN

has written many novels for young readers as well as for adults. She speed walks, works out with weights and enjoys ballroom dancing for exercise, stress reduction and pleasure. Her children are now grown. She lives in Maryland with her husband, Bill, and her writing companion—Sunny, a lovable terrier-mix adopted from a shelter.

Having worked as a hospital switchboard operator, department store sales associate, bank clerk and elementary school teacher, she now splits her days between writing her own books and teaching fiction writing at two local colleges and through a correspondence course. She enjoys helping new writers get a start and speaks "at the drop of a hat" at writers' conferences, libraries and schools across the country.

A Note To My Readers

Although the country of Elbia, her citizens and
Prince Jacob are products of my fantasy-loving
imagination, real monarchies, castles and handsome
princes do exist in our modern world. Liechtenstein's
Hereditary Prince Alois is a tennis buff and resides in
beautiful Vaduz Castle. Monaco's Crown Prince Albert—
who is into judo, fencing and theater—has a reputation
as a charming playboy. Luxembourg looks to
His Royal Highness Prince Henri, an avid sailor and
music lover, for guidance into the next century. He lives
in the breathtaking Château of Fischbach. Denmark's
Crown Prince Frederik, passionate about skiing and
driving fast cars, attended Harvard University in the U.S.
The Netherlands, Spain, Norway, Belgium and Sweden
also boast dashing royals. They all possess vast fortunes
to share with the lucky women who steal their hearts.

One

Time was running out, and Jacob knew it.

In all the world, there was precious little his money couldn't buy. Happiness itself had seemed within his purchasing power. He'd used the von Austerand fortune for twenty-nine years to satisfy his whims, lusts, real and imagined needs. Now the fun was coming to an end.

"Damn!" he growled, crumpling the message and letting it fall from his fist into the blue-gray water lapping the hull of the sleek motor yacht. A brilliant orange September sun was already halfway up a cloudless sky. It beamed down on the snug cove nestled in the Connecticut shoreline, where the *Queen Elise* had anchored the night before.

"Bad news, Your Royal Highness?" a voice colored by a deep British accent asked from behind him.

"The worst, Thomas. The worst."

"The king? He's had another stroke, has he?"

Jacob swung around to face his bodyguard, who doubled as chauffeur, private secretary and self-proclaimed social adviser. Thomas was also his closest—some claimed only—true friend. Anger frothed up inside Jacob. The heat generated by his turbulent mood made his head hurt far worse than the hangover he'd woken with should have.

"My father is in better health than most of his cabinet—better than I am, at this moment." He gingerly pressed the heel of one hand to his forehead, as if to hold its contents securely in place.

"I've prepared a pitcher of Bloody Marys in the galley, Your Royal Highness. Shall I bring it?"

"Knock off the 'Your Highness' crap," Jacob snapped. "You only do that when some reporter is around to hear, or when you're irritated with me."

"As you wish, Sir," Thomas said with a shadow of a smile. "Shall I bring the beverage?"

"No." Jacob shook his head, then groaned at the wave of dizziness the motion produced. "No, it will wear off soon enough. Black coffee would be better."

When Thomas returned with a steaming mug of fragrant dark java, Jacob took a quick sip, then three more…and the world seemed to steady itself. Somewhat. They stood for a while as crew members in white T-shirts and canvas pants bustled around them, then finally disappeared below the polished decks of the *Queen Elise*. The luxurious two-hundred-foot, ocean-going yacht had been a present from his father for his sixteenth birthday. Whenever Jacob could get away for a while, it was his chosen home. But this morning it seemed little comfort to him.

"You deserve that hangover after last night," Thomas commented dryly, as he stood at the rail, smoking a thick black cigar.

"I suppose." Jacob sighed. Aside from his father and Frederik—the old man's chief adviser, who had been with the family since before Jacob's birth—Thomas was the only person who wasn't intimidated by Jacob's money and title. Thomas never pulled punches. And his father never gave up when he wanted something.

What the King of Elbia now wanted…no, *demanded*, was that his only son marry by Christmas, only months away now. Just because he, Karl von Austerand, had been forced to wed before his thirtieth year and his father before him...and his grandfather before that. For over five hundred years the crown princes of Elbia, a tiny European country even smaller than Liechtenstein, had dutifully followed the laws of succession. Now it was Jacob's turn, and he viewed the prospect of a political marriage as medieval idiocy, a trap he had always somehow meant to elude. But now the time had come...and there seemed no way out that wouldn't cost him his inheritance.

"He's sticking to his guns, Thomas," Jacob muttered, gripping the polished brass railing until his knuckles ached. He leaned over the yacht's side to watch white-tipped swells lap the hull. "He says I've had plenty of time to choose a suitable wife. *That*—" he gestured to where the sheet of paper had submerged "—was his latest list of young ladies he deems equal to the task of becoming Elbia's next queen."

Thomas stepped to the young prince's side. "You knew this day would come. This is no surprise."

"Yes. But it always seemed so far away...before now."

"As the sole heir to the throne of Elbia, you must provide an heir," Thomas said softly. "If the von Austerand line were to end...your country would perish." Thomas had always been and would always be an Englishman, but he nevertheless acted protective of his employer's homeland...just as he felt protective of his employer.

Jacob raked a hand through his glistening black hair and glared at the beach. He knew what Thomas said was true. He'd been tormented for most of his adult years by guilt at the thought, but his natural willfulness fought tradition.

A pearly gray-and-white seagull swooped from the sky and soared above them on a warm air current, rising effortlessly with it. Jacob's thoughts wheeled with the bird. He had ordered the yacht to anchor late the previous night in Long Island Sound, after dropping off the last of his guests this side of New York City. Something had drawn him back to this place. Something had made him want to come here again, if only to be alone for a little while and watch the sun rise from this familiar curve of sand and rocks called Nanticoke Bay.

A slender ribbon of peace stretched over his frustration and anger. His grip relaxed on the handrail. The tension knotting his neck slowly released. He breathed in the salty air.

The geography was so different here from landlocked Elbia. The tiny eastern European country had survived German aggression during two world wars and Russian intimidation in the cold war that followed. Elbia, like Monaco and Liechtenstein and only a handful of other modern countries, remained a monarchy, an anachronism in today's high-tech world. As Thomas had so wisely stated, only his country's traditions separated her from becoming absorbed by larger countries or falling into impoverishment. She offered little in the way of valuable resources. She had no oil, no diamonds, no major crops or industries. Her borders included neither a port on open water nor easy access to other rich lands. But she did possess spectacular lakes, breathtaking mountains and ancient castles of unparalleled magnificence. Tourism kept Elbia alive, but without the glamour of the royals and the glitter of the many annual events in her capital city to attract the thousands of visitors who came each year she would be ruined.

Jacob pressed his fingertips against his temples and closed his eyes. "The bottom line is, the king says I must return and take a bride. Immediately. That piece of paper listed his personal top ten choices."

"And?" Thomas asked, an amused lilt in his voice.

"I want *none* of them."

"If they are the same young ladies your father has mentioned before, each is quite agreeable. Of royal blood...well-moneyed families...socially flawless... Several are quite beautiful."

"Then *you* marry them." Jacob waved an impatient hand. He finished his coffee and tossed the mug down on a chaise that had been occupied by a New York actress with exceptionally long legs and a willing smile the night before. "They leave me cold."

"Nevertheless, you've had...shall we say, relations with several of the ladies, I believe."

"I've slept with dozens of women in nearly every country in the world," Jacob stated flatly. "Having sex with a woman doesn't make her someone I'd want to live with for the rest of my life."

Thomas laid a hand on the prince's shoulder. His calm tan-colored eyes observed him from above rotund cheeks and a tidily trimmed Henry VIII beard. "Other men have fulfilled far more distasteful obligations on their countries' behalf," he commented gently.

Jacob nodded. "Don't get me wrong. I've always understood my duty, and I intended to do it when the time came. But now that it's here—damn it, I can't! I don't know why, but I *can't*." He hesitated. "There *was* one...once...but she—"

"One? A woman?" Thomas's eyes brightened.

"Yes. She was special. She was..." What exactly had she been to him during that summer over two years ago? The American girl with the enormous blue-green eyes and hair that had flowed like pale champagne to her shoulders. She had been sweet, simple, loving—and he had found himself utterly charmed by her. No woman had affected him so deeply before or since.

But she was a commoner—and an American on top of that, which was even worse in his father's eyes. Jacob had known, even as they'd lain in each others' arms, he'd have to leave her. It had been the hardest single moment of his life, walking away from her bed that night. Just leaving. Without so much as a goodbye. Without explaining to her who he really was and why he couldn't stay with her.

He'd been a physical and emotional mess for weeks after. But then he'd returned to school and forced himself to concentrate on his studies, which were grueling at the graduate level, and the months had passed. He'd survived.

The only problem was, his relationships with women had

changed in a troubling way. More than two years after he'd left her, he still didn't feel in another woman's arms the sweet and total satisfaction he'd found in hers.

Jacob turned his gaze on the stony line of beach, glowing amber in the autumn sun. The water was still warm enough for swimming, but it wouldn't be for long with winter approaching.

"This woman," Thomas began cautiously. "Is she why we came here last night, when it would have been easier to dock in Greenwich?"

Jacob scowled. He dropped his head in a reluctant nod. "Her name was Allison," he whispered. The sea breeze pulled the syllables from his lips, whisking them away. He hadn't spoken her name since the night he'd left, but he'd thought of her often. Too often.

"Is she not a possible wife?" Thomas asked.

"No." Jacob let out a raspy laugh. "She was as far from princess material as any woman could be. My father would never allow it."

"I see." Thomas drew a deep breath. "Do you intend to see her again?"

Jacob squinted at the row of beachfront cottages, so perfectly New England with their white clapboard fronts, breezy porches and dark green storm shutters. "Yes," he said firmly. "I need to see her just once more. Then I'll stop obsessing about her, comparing other women to her. She couldn't be as..." He struggled to put his thoughts into words. "I don't know what she was any more. She's just clogging up my mind with ridiculous thoughts!" He lashed out angrily, bringing his fist down violently on the brass rail in front of them. "She's unfinished business, Thomas. That's all she is. I'll find her—she lives in Nanticoke. One more time, just to get her out of my blood."

"You mean, you'll have another affair with her?"

"If that's what it takes," Jacob snapped. "Then I'll return to Elbia and decide what must be done."

* * *

It hadn't been the worst day of her life, but it hadn't been the best, either.

When Allison Collins had left for work that morning, little Cray was running a fever and crying fretfully, clinging to her as she tried to escape through the front door. Her sister, Diane, had her hands full with her own three kids—trying to get two of them off to catch their bus for school, while dressing the third. Within a few minutes her three day-care children would arrive, and she'd have a full house again. Tending a sick fifteen-month-old baby wouldn't make her day any easier.

"I'm sorry. I shouldn't leave Cray with you when he's like this," Allison apologized.

"Don't start on the guilt trips again," Diane said. "He's just going through a clingy stage. I'll give him some Tempra and he'll be fine ten minutes after you leave."

"I don't know, maybe I should take the day off and keep him at home." That sounded so good. More days than not, it was what Allison wanted to do anyway. Every time she left Cray, she felt as if a vital part of her were being torn from her body. She missed being with him, but what was a single mom to do? She was lucky Diane had been willing to add him to her houseful of little ones at half her usual fee. Day care was so expensive, and a librarian's salary in a matchbox town like Nanticoke didn't go far.

Their parents had moved to Florida, when they'd retired five years earlier, leaving the beach house to Allison. She felt grateful for being able to stay there. She still had to pay taxes on the property and manage utilities, food, clothing, medical bills and other necessities. Somehow, she squeezed out the pennies and stayed out of debt—but just barely. She wouldn't have minded all that much. It seemed a lot of families had to struggle to make ends meet, these days. But she never felt as if she had enough time for Cray, and that she did mind.

At least they had a roof over their heads, she reflected. And Cray was a healthy, normal baby. Perhaps that was why leaving him when he wasn't feeling well was so difficult for her. He didn't seem himself. She felt like a heartless witch for deserting him when he needed her.

Finally, she extricated herself from Cray's chubby fingers and made a dash through the kitchen. Before the storm door slammed shut, she could hear his wails of protest. Biting down on her lower lip, she threw herself into her little compact car and fled.

Her morning story-time group of elementary school children was waiting for her in a circle on the carpet when she arrived. She snatched up the two books she'd prepared the previous day and read with as much enthusiasm as she could muster, still exhausted from being up most of the night with Cray.

After the children left, she switched to her other job—cataloging new contributions to the library's collection of first editions. A few hours later, she covered for other staff members during their lunch breaks. Afternoons, following school dismissal, were always busy. The children's corner often turned into an informal baby-sitting service when parents dropped off their kids and left to do errands. It was a practice the staff was trying to stop, since youngsters left unattended sometimes got out of hand and required supervision from staff members who should have been helping patrons locate books or research materials.

By the time five o'clock rolled around, Allison was barely able to see through the dense cloud of fatigue that enclosed her.

"You look beat," Miriam, one of the senior volunteers, remarked as Allison passed her at the checkout desk.

"All I want to do is pick up my baby, go home and sit on the porch with a tall glass of iced tea," she murmured without slowing down. She didn't even have enough energy for a decent conversation.

Tripping wearily down the library's steps, Allison watched the worn granite slabs pass beneath her feet. Chips of color—quartz, feldspar, obsidian, she thought vaguely. Home...just get me home, car. She hoped she had enough gas.

"Alli?"

She froze where she stood on the bottom step. A flash of ice replaced the warm blood flowing through her veins. But her cheeks immediately flamed up. She didn't need to lift her eyes to place the rich baritone colored with the faintest Germanic and British overtones. Her heart crawled into her throat. Her hand flew up to cover her mouth before the cry of dismay working its way to her lips could escape.

Only after taking four controlled full breaths, did Allison dare look up...and up...and up into the blue-black eyes of the man standing in front of her. "Hello, Jay," she said, amazed at the control she was able to exert over her own voice.

He smiled.

She frowned.

"Not happy to see me?" he asked.

"Why should I be?" she clipped out. Stepping to one side, she tried to dodge around him, but he mirrored her side step, effectively blocking her path to her car.

He stood there, looking confident and handsome in casual tan chinos that hugged his hips and a turquoise golf shirt. The muscles of his chest stretched the fabric when he drew a deep breath.

"We were pretty good friends once," he pointed out. His eyes teased, reflecting hidden meanings she understood all too easily.

Lord, she thought, after all these months, how can he make me feel like this? "That was a long time ago," she stated crisply. "Now I have to get home."

His glance dropped to her left hand, then flashed back up to her face, looking satisfied. "I see you haven't married, either."

"Why should I?" She faked to the left. He fell for it. She slipped past him and sprinted for her car, calling over her shoulder, "I can just keep on having meaningless affairs with guys like you! Great sex, no commitments, no responsibilities." She didn't care if she sounded bitter. She wanted to make him go away. Forever.

She was running now, and so were her thoughts. They rushed at her, in troubling abandon as she bounded across the parking lot. Why had he come back? *Why?* Just when she thought she'd moved on to another part of her life— one without painful memories of him and how it had felt in those heady, wonderful weeks he'd stayed with her at the beach house. What a fool he'd made of her!

She reached her car, jammed the key in the lock. A wide hand sprinkled with dark hair fell over hers, stopping her from turning the key.

"Don't you dare touch me," she ground out between clenched teeth. "I swear, if you—"

He immediately lifted his offending hand and held it up for her to see, as if demonstrating its innocence. "Fine. I won't touch you. I just want to talk."

"No."

"Why not?"

She spun around and glared at him. "Why not? We were lovers for nearly two months, Jay! Then you pulled a disappearing act. Or don't you remember?"

"I remember," he said softly. For a second, she thought she saw a tender radiance lighten his dark eyes. But before she could be sure, it was gone. He looked hardened, determined again.

"Then you also must remember that you didn't leave a note, you didn't tell me you wouldn't be back the next night, you never said goodbye. You just walked out of my life." She fixed him with a challenging glare, daring him to deny any of it.

"I…" He shrugged and let out a halfhearted laugh. "Guess I didn't know how to say, 'so long.'"

"Yeah, right," she snapped. Shoving him hard in the chest, she took advantage of his startled attempt to regain his balance. Allison swung open the car door and dove into the steamy interior. The sun had been strong all afternoon, heating up the closed vehicle, and the air-conditioning hadn't worked in three years. The ride home would be stifling, but at least she'd be on her own turf, where she could pull herself together.

"Alli, stop!" His angry shout rocked her, even through the barrier of glass.

Instinctively, she cringed, as he yanked open the door and hauled her into the sea air as easily as if she'd been a sack of groceries. She was shaking as he backed her against the car, then stood so close she couldn't maneuver to break free again.

"What do you want from me?" she shouted, her voice breaking as tears clung to her pale lashes.

He had already taken so much from her. He'd been the first man she'd ever let touch her like that. Her first love. Her only, to this day. And he'd left her carrying his baby inside her. The heartbreak of his desertion had been almost too much for her to bear.

Unloved. Abandoned. He'd left her alone, to care for a fragile life—the baby they'd created on an amorous night on the beach, when she'd believed with all her heart that he loved her.

After he left and she discovered she was pregnant, she'd made the necessary decisions and preparations, and kept herself busy. She told herself if she could just get through that one year, she could handle anything life threw at her. She hadn't bargained on ever again having to face the man who had done his best to destroy her life.

"I just want to do something nice for you," he said stiffly.

Something told her he'd practiced that line. Suspicious, she squinted up at him. "The nicest thing you can do for me, Jay, is stay out of my life."

"Uh-uh." He shook his head; the breeze off the ocean caught the one stray black curl over his forehead and played with it. His shadowed eyes fixed steadily on hers.

She was terrified that their closeness was exciting him. She contemplated screaming for help, then dismissed the idea. Something about the little-boy glint in his eyes made her slightly more curious than afraid.

"Walk with me on the beach," he said. "I have something to tell you. I guarantee you'll like it."

She sighed and cast him a rueful glance. "Is this the only way to get rid of you?"

"Only way." He grinned.

"I must be out of my mind," she mumbled. "All right. Ten minutes walking on the beach, then I'm out of here. And so are you."

"I'll let you decide about that after I've had my say," he said, stepping back to let her move away from the car. "Hey, wait up!"

She was already sprinting across the road, toward the beach. He had to take enormous strides to keep up with her energetic pace. She was used to speed-walking for exercising, while pushing Cray's stroller ahead of her. And now she felt the urge to move, fast.

The beach hugged Long Island Sound and formed a cup-shaped cove along the coast, sheltering tidal pools of periwinkles, miniature crabs and silvery fish smaller than her little finger, among clumps of shiny green and brown kelp. Soaring gulls and sea terns pecked among glassy-smooth pebbles, wave-polished fragments of colored glass and chunks of artfully deformed driftwood. At this time of year, all the sunbathers had left.

Allison breathed in the air, thick with brine. The cries of the sea birds nearly drowned out the steady slosh and scrape of the waves on the stony beach. As always, the ocean had a calming effect on her, taking her temper down a notch and returning a portion of her sanity. I don't have to let this jerk rattle me, she told herself. I can simply tell him the time we spent together was fun but I'm not interested in taking up where we left off.

Why give him the satisfaction of discovering how much he'd meant to her?

She could even be a little creative, claim she had a boyfriend. Or tell him she was married and had a baby... *No,* she couldn't do that! She wouldn't dare give him enough information to let him guess the truth.

Allison stopped halfway between the sidewalk and the ocean, her body trembling at the thought of how close she'd come to making a horrible mistake. It was dangerous to tell him anything of what had happened after he'd left. She stared down at the damp grains of sand, then braced her fists on her hips and looked out across the water, hoping he'd say what he'd come to say quickly. Two sailboats played among the white caps offshore. The marina, in the next cove, was full of pleasure boats, large and small. In another month, nearly all would have been pulled out for winter storage. Anchored a little apart from the other craft was a long, low white ship that must have been three times the size of the largest yacht in the marina. It floated majestically, barely moving on the water, as if unconcerned with waves or wind.

"Oh, my," she let out, unintentionally.

He stopped behind her. "She's something, isn't she?"

Allison nodded. "I don't think I've ever seen anything that big in Nanticoke Cove."

"She's called the *Queen Elise*. She can cross the Atlantic a whole day faster than the *QE2*."

Allison let her glance drift downward from the immense yacht to stare at the wavelets rippling closest to her feet. "You're full of it, Jay."

He laughed out loud this time. "What?"

"You heard me. You have no idea what the name of that ship is. You're just experimenting with another pickup line."

"I'm not, Alli. Honest."

"Baloney!" She couldn't help sounding spiteful now, couldn't pretend to be callous and modern about relationships. "Two years ago, you told me you were a graduate student on summer break. You claimed you were studying for your master's degree in political science at Yale." New Haven was less than an hour's drive to the east, along the coast of Connecticut, so his story had seemed reasonable to her.

"I was."

"Don't lie, Jay!" she shouted, spinning around to face him. Her rage nearly made it impossible for her to form words. "You never were a student at Yale," she choked out. "I know because I checked."

He stared mutely at her.

She was close to tears now, as she remembered how desperate she had been to contact him. Even if he hadn't wanted to come back to her, she'd wanted to tell him about the baby. She'd been so confused, so frightened and alone. But he hadn't been there for her. In the end, all she'd wanted was to let him hear her decision—that she intended to keep their child. Maybe he had somehow guessed he'd impregnated her, and that was why he'd left. But on the more likely chance that he hadn't known, her strong sense of fairness demanded she tell him that he was going to be a father. Then he could make his own decision about taking on the responsibility or not.

"Shut up!" Allison said when he started to open his mouth. "I'll save you the trouble of asking. I called the college registrar's office and argued with three different clerks, insisting there must be a Jay Thomas in the student body. But they said no one under that name was registered."

He looked more amazed than angry. "You did that? You actually tried to track me down?"

She glared at him.

"Ouch," he said, and looked out at the water.

"You deceived me, Jay. You used me. All you wanted was a summer fling. And I was too naive to guess that what we were doing could be that ordinary and simple."

"I'm sorry," he said tightly. "That's one reason I came back…to apologize for the way I treated you. I want to make it up to you. Come out with me for dinner."

She threw up her hands, veered away from him, and started marching down the beach. She was so angry she could have strangled him. Or better yet, put a blunt instrument to good use.

"Incredible," she muttered to herself. The man steals

your heart, relieves you of your virginity, and ditches you after getting you pregnant…then he wants to buy you a meal and make nice. She knew she couldn't have said another word to him, she was so furious. The words would have vaporized like steam from her lips.

"Alli!" he shouted after her. "Listen to me!"

She ignored him, kept on walking, the sand sifting into her shoes, between her toes, making each step feel gritty and slow-motion awkward.

A hand roughly gripped her arm, taking her by surprise. She hadn't heard him chasing her. She recovered and faced him, her shoulders ratcheted back, her eyes brittle with emotion, seething with hatred. But her chin trembled, giving her away. She blinked back hot tears.

"Listen…" he hissed at her, and started to say something more. But he changed his mind and quickly bent down to press his lips over hers.

The heat and intensity of his kiss shocked her. It was the last thing she'd expected from a runaway boyfriend who'd lied his way into her heart, then disappeared without a trace. Why was he doing this to her?

Allison was trembling from head to foot when his lips finally brushed away from hers. His grip on her wrist loosened, but he closed his muscular arms around her in a warm embrace. She thought for a brief moment how strange his body felt, wrapped around hers, as if he was holding himself up as much as he was restraining her from running away again.

He kept her there, pinned tightly against his chest, as he began talking in his perfect English with the almost indistinguishable hint of an accent that had intrigued her from their first meeting. "Please just let me explain and try to do this right, for a change." He didn't wait for her response. "Yes, I lied. But not about being a grad student at Yale. I *was* enrolled there…under a different name."

"Your name isn't Jay?"

"My American friends sometimes called me that. Occasionally, it suited other situations. My name's Jacob."

"Jacob," she repeated, feeling the need to test out the sounds. The name suited him, although why, she couldn't have said. "Jacob Thomas?"

"No." He hesitated, and she sensed a growing tension in his neck and arms, as if he was having second thoughts about continuing. "Do you read the gossip columns in grocery store tabloids?" he asked.

She blinked up at him, wondering what one thing had to do with the other. "No, why do you—"

"What about newspapers?"

"The front page and local news, occasionally. I don't have a lot of reading time with—" She stopped herself from adding, *with a full-time job and an infant to raise.*

He sighed and adjusted his hold on her, and she began to wonder if he actually feared she'd take a swing at him if he released her. "Promise you'll let me finish."

She felt like screaming. "Just say what's on your mind, Jacob, or whoever the hell you are, and let me get on with my life!"

He took a deep breath that she could feel through her ribs, pressed against his.

"My real name, my entire legal name as it appears on my birth certificate is—His Royal Highness, Jacob Phillipe Mark von Austerand, Crown Prince of Elbia. That yacht out there is mine, and I want you to have dinner with me on it, tonight."

Allison closed her eyes, feeling numb from head to toe. She said nothing, didn't move an inch. After a minute Jacob dropped his arms and stepped back to observe her expression. She focused on the strong angles of his face, which seemed perfectly composed and serious. Pursing her lips, she folded her arms over her chest and smiled sweetly up at him.

He tentatively lifted one corner of his lips in response.

"And I am Queen Elizabeth," she stated calmly. "Get a life, Jay."

Before he could reply, she was jogging up over a sand dune, toward the road. The last she saw of him, he was staring after her, a stunned expression on his handsome face.

Two

Crown prince, indeed. "A college grad like you ought to be able to come up with a better line than that!" Allison huffed as she threw herself into her car and drove toward Diane's house.

Maybe she'd hang around for an hour or two, help her sister with the day-care kids. She had been exhausted when she left the library, but her fury had energized her. If Cray was feeling better, she could give Diane a hand with the chores. Besides, delaying her return to the beach house might be wise. If Jay was feeling particularly pigheaded, he might try to intercept her again at her home. She didn't think Jay...Jacob...whoever, would remember where her sister lived.

Allison pulled up in front of the tidy driftwood gray Cape Cod three blocks back of the water and halfway across town. She didn't lock the car, but on second thought took the keys with her. Nanticoke was a small, peaceful town, but she didn't believe in tempting fate or some teenager looking for a joyride. Just last week, two fifteen-year-olds too lazy to walk to school had "borrowed" her neighbor's car. The police had found it parked in the high school parking lot. Dumb kids.

She let herself in through the kitchen door without knocking, plucked an apple from the red plastic bowl on the table and bounced down the cellar stairs to the finished rec room where Diane spent most of her days with her charges.

The children were clustered around her, sitting on a mat on the floor, while Diane read to them from a picture book with a comical bear on the cover. Allison crossed her ankles and lowered herself to the floor, munching on her apple, feeling her pulse slow to a calmer pace. Cray spotted her and pushed himself up from the floor. He toddled over, grinning and chattering unintelligibly, and trustingly dropped into her lap.

Allison wrapped her arms around her little boy and hugged him, rocking back and forth. "You make everything all right, you know that?" she whispered into the feathery tufts of dark hair above his ear.

He gurgled contentedly as she swept stray bangs off his forehead. His skin felt cool and the feverish glaze over his eyes was gone. She was relieved to see him looking better.

After the story was over, Diane deposited each child in a high chair. Allison helped her pour juice and pass out pretzels for a final snack of the day. She felt herself gear down another notch and chuckled softly. Times like this, she thought, a girl really has to keep her sense of humor.

"What's so funny?" Diane asked.

"Hard to explain," Allison replied, shaking her head. "You wouldn't believe me anyway."

"Try me."

She drew a long breath. "I saw Cray's father."

Diane dropped the bag of pretzels. Crumbs scattered across the playroom floor. "Jay?" Her cheeks flushed red and her eyes narrowed dangerously. "That creep. The nerve of him crawling back now. What does he want?"

"I'm not sure," Allison said, thoughtfully. "I wouldn't

trust him under the best of conditions. But he told me a weird story about his being a prince and living on a yacht." She laughed out loud. "Prince of Elbia! You'd think he could come up with something more believable, if he wanted to impress a girl."

Diane stooped to pick up the plastic bag that had split down one side. "Elbia? Isn't that the postage-stamp-size country near Austria that's been in the news lately?"

Allison shrugged. "Who knows. I don't have time to keep up with international politics these days. Every spare moment I've either been cataloging the new books or taking care of Cray. Last Sunday, I even took him with me while I worked overtime."

"Wait here," Diane said. "Pass out another round of goodies, if there's enough." She shoved the bag into Allison's hands.

A minute later she was back downstairs with a broom in one hand, a full pitcher of juice in the other and the *New York Times* tucked under one arm. She set down the pitcher and broom, and spread the paper on the table. "I know I heard something about a meeting at the United Nations, an Eastern European coalition...something like that." She frantically flipped pages while Allison looked over her shoulder, wondering if her sister had gone mad. "The president was going to meet with delegates. One was this young..." She stopped flipping and pointed triumphantly at a photograph in the middle of the right-hand page. "There. Crown Prince Jacob von Austerand. Gee, I would never have connected him with some grad student from Connecticut but..." She wrinkled her nose, considering. "Alli, he *does* look a lot like Jay...with a couple of years under his belt."

Allison snatched up the newspaper section. She stared at the black-and-white UPI photo of three men in expensive business suits. The tall wide-shouldered one shaking hands with the President of the United States was Jay, no doubt about it.

Her eyes dropped quickly to the caption, and she read it

out loud. "Prince Jacob von Austerand of Elbia congratulates the president after his speech before the Eastern Unity Conference on Tuesday."

"The creep," Diane muttered, picking up the broom to sweep violently at the tile floor. "Egotistical playboy. People with money make me sick. They think they can do anything they want...doesn't matter who gets hurt."

Allison frowned at her sister, trying to put together the pieces of a puzzle, for which she seemed to have only half the pieces. Now that she focused on the scraps of news she'd heard over the radio or glimpsed on TV, she remembered hearing things about a playboy prince. He'd been linked romantically with Hollywood actresses, wealthy socialites, even one female rock singer. Was that Jay...Jacob? If so, how had *she* fit in with all those glamorous women?

"I—I can't believe he's who he says he is," she stammered, her voice rising in panic. "Diane? How could I not have known? The man's a public figure...a celebrity!"

Diane stopped sweeping and patted her arm. "Why would you know? Even if someone recognized him, he could easily pretend he just looked like the prince. Apparently, he likes playing games with women. He has a pretty wild reputation, you know."

"I know...of course, I know. He's right up there with the Kennedys and the British royals." Allison suddenly felt deflated, hollow inside. She shook her head. "So I was just another amusing affair for him...."

"Apparently," Diane said, using a wet cloth to wipe crumbs from a toddler's chubby cheeks. "Hey, consider yourself lucky. Now that you know the truth, it should be that much easier to put the jerk out of your mind."

"He *was* out of my mind, until he showed up at the library today."

"Was he? Out of your mind, that is." Diane cast her a skeptical look. "It's not like you've been dating anyone else in the two-plus years since he disappeared."

"That's not because I'm hung up on him," Allison insisted. "I just have to be more careful who I see, now that Cray's around."

"Right." Diane rolled her eyes. "So, are you going to see him? Jacob?"

"Are you crazy? Of course, I'm not going to see him. There's nothing that could make me set foot on that yacht or anywhere else he happens to be."

The doorbell rang at precisely 7:00 p.m. that evening. When Allison answered it, a man in a brown delivery-service uniform was standing on her front step, holding a large box in front of his face.

"Yes?" she asked, certain there had been a mistake. She hadn't ordered anything by mail recently.

"Miss Allison Collins?"

She frowned, for the first few seconds unable to place the voice. "Jacob?"

He lowered the box and rested his chin on it, to gaze at her with a wicked smile.

"What are you doing here?"

"Delivering a package," he said simply. "It's pretty heavy. I'd better bring it inside for you."

He pushed past her into the living room, stopping to look around when he reached the middle of the room. "Cozy. I remember your colonial decor—not bad reproductions."

Allison trailed after him, sputtering her exasperation. "Get out of here this minute! Take whatever's in that box with you."

"Oh, you wouldn't want me to do that," he responded and set the package down on her mother's rock maple coffee table. "You wouldn't have anything to wear to the party tomorrow night, if I took it away."

She planted her feet at shoulders' width, folded her arms across her chest, and glared at him. "What party?"

"The one I'm throwing on the *Queen Elise* tomorrow night. You're invited." He removed the stiff-brimmed uniform cap and combed his fingers through thick black waves. "Aren't you going to open it?" He nudged his chin toward the box.

Allison lost her last strand of self-control. "No!" she shouted, rushing at him. "I want you out of my house...out of my life...out, out, out...*now!*"

He fell back a step, observing her as if she were a rare animal, recently captured but not yet identified...and certainly not tamed.

"Out!" she screamed.

A piercing wail rose above her voice.

Oh, no, she thought. Not now, Cray. Why hadn't she been more careful to keep her voice down?

Jacob turned toward the hallway, his eyebrows arched, questioning. "What's that?"

Allison thought of a half dozen lies on the spot. *It's my sister's child; I'm baby-sitting. That's the neighbor's baby. The TV is on in the bedroom.* None of them worked.

"That's my son," she said finally. "Now, if you'll leave, I'll go and take care of him."

Jacob scowled. "Why didn't you tell me you were married?"

"I'm not."

"I see." He took a step back. Somewhere among the planes of his face, a hardness grew and solidified. "I should have known a pretty woman like you wouldn't be alone for long." His eyes wandered toward the hallway. "That doesn't sound like an infant's cry."

"Cray is fifteen months old, if you must know," she said without thinking. Immediately, she wished she hadn't. The man wasn't stupid.

"Fifteen months?"

She followed the tiny motions of his eyes, which grew faster by the second.

"I'd like you to leave now," she said stiffly, desperate to get him out of the house, away from her son. She was having trouble breathing. "I have to get Cray settled down for the night. He hasn't been feeling well."

"Who is the father?" Jacob asked, his voice taut with emotion.

Allison leveled her sternest look at him. "*That* is none of your business. Go. Leave!"

The levels of emotion that crossed Jacob's face were more frightening than any words he might have spoken. Instead of turning toward the door, he lurched forward, stopping inches from where she stood. His hands shot forward, vised her shoulders. He glared down at her, his eyes hot, bright chips of obsidian—blacker than black.

"I'll leave after you tell me the name of the father."

"Maybe I just don't know." She couldn't help baiting him. He deserved it, didn't he?

"I'm supposed to believe that around the time we were together, you were sleeping with a handful of other men, too?"

"Why not?" she challenged him. "I could have been."

His hands tightened painfully on her shoulders. "You're not that kind of woman."

Cray was still crying from the back room, but no longer urgently.

"How would you know?" she said, her eyes falling away from his, despite her determination to give as good as she got. "You didn't hang around long enough to get to know me."

"I knew you well enough, Alli." Jacob bent over her, capturing her eyes once more with his. "I knew you inside and out—every inch of your body, every corner of your sweet, generous soul."

In one quick move, he released her shoulders but enclosed her in his arms. She could feel the heat of his body through their clothing. His lean, hard strength met her soft curves. He pressed her to him, and she could feel that he was aroused. Knowing that embarrassed her.

But not enough to make her struggle to be released. Some secret need or inner force kept her from fighting him. It had been so long, so very long since a man had held her. There had been a few dinners or group movie dates, arranged by Diane or one of her girlfriends. But she hadn't encouraged a second meeting or allowed herself to be alone with a man. Now she realized how much she'd missed the intoxicating sensations that were rushing through her body.

Cray's cries had turned to sleepy whimpers. She wished he'd let out a long, hearty scream to give her an excuse for breaking out of Jacob's arms. She wished she had more willpower than she seemed to have at the moment. She wished...wished that Jacob would stop doing whatever it was he was doing.

His thumb stroked the side of her breast through her cotton sweater. Fiery tongues licked through her, making her knees feel weak. "Don't do that," she whispered.

"Tell me the name of the baby's father?" Jacob said, his voice rumbling in his chest, vibrating against hers.

"I—I can't."

"You can't. That's different from you don't know."

Allison felt incapable of accomplishing anything more demanding than continuing to breathe in and out. And she wasn't too sure she could keep that up for much longer. She was powerless to mold her thoughts into words.

"I can't, Jay...Jacob...don't make me..."

"Make you what?" His lips were less than an inch from hers. She could taste the spicy tang of his breath passing between them, smell subtle traces of male perspiration, feel a tension within his body that seemed to radiate through his skin and slip beneath hers.

She closed her eyes, steeling herself with a moment of darkness and silence, shutting herself off from him visually, although she felt him all around her.

"Jacob, he's all I have. You left. Please stay away. I can't deal with this."

She felt all the strength rush out of the man. His hands dropped away from her and he stepped back. "My God," he breathed. "He *is* my child."

Her eyes flew open in sudden terror. "No! He's mine, *just mine* and no one else's."

Jacob stared at her as if he still didn't believe what he

knew in his soul must be true. "*Someone* is that child's father. Let me see him. I'll know."

"No!" she shouted. "Get out. Get out or I'll call the police. I swear I will!"

He reached out for her, but she dodged away. A terror unlike any she'd ever experienced raced through her, blinding her to all thoughts but one. If Jacob was who he claimed to be—the man whose picture Diane had showed her in the newspaper—he had power and money enough to do anything he wished. Anything.

That included taking her child away from her, if he could prove he was Cray's father. Until this moment, it hadn't occurred to her that she might be in real danger of losing Cray. She'd believed all she had to fear was another bruising to her heart and pride.

This was worse, far worse.

"Listen to me, Alli," Jacob begged in a hoarse whisper. "No one is going to hurt you or that baby. You have my word."

Maybe it was because she heard a subtle undercurrent of fear in his voice that she felt comforted. She kept her distance but turned toward him. His dark eyes looked sad, confused. This was all new to him. As he stood there, he must have been absorbing the various concepts attached to fatherhood, one at a time, but very rapidly. She'd had fifteen months to become comfortable with being a mother.

Jacob spoke to her again, his voice uneven. "I'm not going to hurt you again. I'm sorry. I didn't know…didn't realize—" He let the unfinished thought go. He turned his head away as if uneasy with meeting her gaze. He blinked at the wall and held himself rigid in the middle of her living room unsure of which way to move, or whether he should move at all.

Allison reached out one hand and touched the arm of her couch. Slowly, she let herself down onto a lumpy cushion, then dropped her head into her hands. "If you mean what you say about not hurting me, you'll leave now," she whispered dully.

"Is that really what you want?"

"Haven't I said so a dozen times?" she moaned. "Just go away...and don't come back."

She heard him pacing the carpet, cursing beneath this breath. She sensed him standing over her, studying her...and she kept her eyes closed, her palms pressed over her eyes, blocking him out as best she could, as she prayed he'd do what she asked.

But when the door closed with a faint, irrevocable click, Allison felt something fragile shatter inside of her.

"Jacob?" she whispered, dropping her hands and staring at the door. "Jacob?"

The rental car was a shiny white Lincoln Continental—plush, smelling new-car pungent, richly upholstered in buff-colored butter-soft leather. Its luxurious interior contrasted sharply with the simple, homey furnishings of Alli's beach house.

Jacob had stood helplessly over her as she collapsed onto the cheap plaid upholstered couch, which looked like something older people might have bought decades earlier and left with the house. Or maybe it was one of Alli's yard-sale treasures. He actually didn't remember it from the summer they'd spent together.

But now he was unable to get the damn colors of the room out of his head. Shades of rust and gold matched the mustard-colored carpet that looked carefully maintained to last another twenty years. Nothing he'd seen in the house was of any real worth, except for a few pieces of antique porcelain displayed on a sideboard. The whole lot would have brought a couple hundred dollars on the auction block—less than the cost of the hand-tailored silk shirt he wore.

Back when they'd been together, she hadn't seemed so different from him. They both loved books. They talked endlessly about their favorite kinds of music, art, literature. She daydreamed about traveling to foreign lands. He'd played along, promising to take her wherever she wanted—Rome, Vienna, Paris, Madrid—not letting on he'd already been to all the places she dreamed of visiting. And she'd laughed at him, never suspecting that he had the power to do all that he said.

Today, she seemed to him to come from another world—one where people proudly pinched pennies to afford new slipcovers, one where a two-bedroom single-bath cottage was large enough to raise a family with three or four kids. One where a young woman's pride and love were worth more than any amount of money.

On top of all that—the existence of the child was a total shock. He had always been so careful. Hadn't his father's closest adviser, Frederik, constantly stressed to a young prince the dangers of unprotected contact with young women? He must have been no more than twelve years old the first time he'd suffered through the lord counselor's tedious lecture. But soon it had come to make more sense to him. Not only was health an issue, there were vast financial and dynastic considerations.

If a young woman appeared on the castle's doorstep with a baby, claiming it had been sired by the crown prince...at the very least, the world press corps would have a field day. But if she could actually *prove* the child was Prince Jacob's bastard, all hell would break loose in Elbia. She'd have to be paid off, and handsomely. A million dollars to silence her and support the child wouldn't be too much.

Jacob understood that his father, his cabinet and royal advisers wouldn't object to his sowing his proverbial oats as long as he did so discreetly, with no embarrassing repercussions. During his late teen years and throughout his twenties, he'd had frequent opportunities to practice discretion. He quickly learned that money and fame were powerful aphrodisiacs. Women were more than willing to share their bodies with him, just to say they'd slept with a real prince. And he was generous during his brief affairs. He bought his lovers expensive gifts—jewelry, cars, expensive clothing. One charming lady had even merited a profitable boutique on the Rue de la Seine in Paris, in return for a few months' companionship. If they were at all disappointed when he left them, they didn't complain. His parting gifts had a consoling effect.

Alli had been different.

The day in June when he'd met her on the beach, he'd somehow sensed she wasn't the kind of girl to be impressed by a title or seeing a lot of cash thrown her way. There was a quality about her that transcended the world he'd come to know. She smiled, and his heart warmed. She laughed, and he felt life was simple and free of the stifling obligations that awaited him back home in Elbia.

Alli loved books and worked in a library. Books had been his only friends as he'd grown up in a cold, friendless castle overlooking the valley of his homeland. He felt good around her. He felt like a normal man—not someone whose destiny was determined at birth, who had no choice in career or home or mate.

He had chosen her for a few weeks of love and friendship and he'd been so happy living in her world, if only for that short time.

Unlike all the other times, he had not told his mistress who he was. He was sure that if he had, Alli wouldn't have become involved with him or allowed him to stay. For then she'd understand he couldn't remain with her, even if he'd wanted to. That was where he'd most cruelly deceived her. He'd known she was falling in love with him. He'd known he was going to have to hurt her. But he hadn't been man enough to stay and see her tears when he said goodbye.

As he thought about these things, Jacob started the car and began driving. He didn't pay much attention to where the road was taking him until he steered into the marina's parking lot. He left the car for the valet to park, waved down the launch and climbed aboard. He pointed at the *Queen Elise,* then stood in the bow, ignoring the pleasant chatter of the young man who piloted the water taxi to the larger ships anchored offshore. All the while, Jacob kicked himself for looking up Alli again.

Before today, he'd been haunted by her in ways he

couldn't have explained to himself and wouldn't have even tried to rationalize for Thomas, Frederik or his father. There had been women after Alli, but they hadn't excited him as she had. Thoughts of her had unexpectedly come to him at the worst possible moments—interfering with his ability to enjoy intimacy or make important decisions that would affect his future.

By seeing her again, he'd hoped to put his head right. Get her out of his system, as he'd told Thomas. She'd be fifty pounds heavier and totally out of shape. She'd have married a brute of a trucker with a pierced nose...be saddled with two whiny brats who, sadly, resembled their beer-guzzling dad.

But she wasn't any of those things. She was as sweet and innocent and perfect as when they'd been together. And she turned him on something fierce whenever they touched, even more so when they'd kissed. He wasn't over her, he thought dismally. Not by a long shot.

But far worse, he'd learned he had a son. And that was a problem he couldn't walk away from.

Alli might swear to him that she'd never make the paternity of her child public knowledge, and she probably would keep that promise. But what if some snoopy reporter got hold of the information despite her vow of silence? What if someone close to Alli decided there was money to be made by selling her secret?

All of that aside, Jacob didn't know if he could be low enough to turn his back on a child he'd created. Just the thought of having a son drew emotions from him he didn't know he had. Pride...concern...responsibility... The others were far too confusing to even begin to analyze.

He slumped against a crate being ferried to one of the boats in the cove as the sleek launch zipped between expensive pleasure boats, heading for the one that dwarfed all the rest, the *Queen Elise*. He remembered he hadn't taken Alli's package with him, then shrugged. What did it matter now? Whether or not she accepted his gift or came to his party was the least of his worries.

* * *

Alli stood over Cray's crib, looking tenderly down at her son as he napped. A wave of such intense emotion washed over her, its force nearly knocked her off of her feet. She loved the little boy, as any mother loved her child. But now she feared for him, as she feared for herself.

Jacob.

Why had he come back?

He had acted surprised when Cray started crying in his bedroom. Had that reaction been an honest one? Or had he known all along that she had given birth to his child?

An icy shiver curled through her. Of course, a man like Jacob had all sorts of ways of keeping track of people. What if he'd been informed of Cray's existence many months ago? What if he was only now getting around to coming to Connecticut to claim his son?

The possibility terrified her.

But there was something wrong with that reasoning, she told herself. If having a son meant anything to him, why had he waited so long? Why hadn't he shown up while she'd been pregnant? During those trying emotional months, she'd been at her weakest. She'd been so very afraid she wouldn't know how to take care of a child, and wouldn't be capable of supporting herself and Cray on her meager pay. If Jacob had known she was about to have his baby, why hadn't he shown up then?

Maybe he was up to something far worse than she'd imagined. He wanted something from her, or he wouldn't have come back. Until she knew exactly what that was, she wouldn't be able to protect herself or her son from him.

After draping a light blanket over Cray and touching his fuzzy little head one last time, Allison slowly made her way out to the kitchen at the back of the house. She brewed herself a cup of hot tea and took it into the living room. There, on the floor, sat the large dark mauve box Jacob had brought earlier.

Allison sat on the couch, staring speculatively at the unmarked package while she sipped her tea. I don't care what's in there, she thought. It's going back.

But how? she asked herself. She could pay someone to take the thing back to him on his stupid boat. But why should she go to the expense when money was already tight? What she should do was shove the unopened box in the trash. That would show him!

But the thrifty New Englander in Allison wouldn't allow her to throw away a perfectly good...perfectly good what? What would she be throwing away?

She glared at the box, imagining something evil and threatening lurking inside the innocent-looking but interestingly colored cardboard. Pandora's box—the classic tease. Why was he doing this to her? Had he intentionally left the thing to torment her, knowing she couldn't stop herself from opening it?

Acting on impulse, Allison set her mug on the coffee table and stood up. She approached the box warily, from the side, as if afraid something alive might leap out of it at any moment, baring its fangs at her. Reaching down, she slipped her fingers inside one flap and tore the box open.

Three

———

Her hands trembling, Allison bent back the four cardboard flaps, then parted layer after layer of distinctive rose-and-gold tissue paper. She recognized the color and pattern of the wrapping materials. They had come from a posh Manhattan clothier. She and Diane had once dared each other to walk through the elegant etched-glass doors, and Diane had treated her to a silk scarf for her birthday that cost twice as much as anything in Allison's closet.

Breathlessly, she reached beneath the crackling sheets of tissue and touched something soft, silky, fluid. She lifted the fabric. Suspended from her fingertips was a pale peacock blue dress of delicate tucks and flounces. It was the most beautiful garment she'd ever seen.

She was furious.

"You son of a—" She stopped herself, remembering Cray, who was within hearing range.

But this dress!

It was both a bribe and a slap in the face. Apparently, Jacob had intended for her to wear his gift to his party. He thought that by giving her something expensive he could persuade her to do whatever he wanted, just as he'd bribed, seduced and sweet-talked countless other women into bed. To him, it was a reflex. Like snapping his fingers to summon a waiter. *Come here. Obey me!*

But this was far, far worse, because in a way he was also saying he doubted she'd have anything decent to wear among polite company. Or—she wouldn't have the sense to dress appropriately for one of his high-society soirees.

Opening her fingers, she let the delicate silk layers drift through them and back into the box. "I'll show you, Your Royal High and Mightiness," she hissed.

Jacob stood in the bow of the *Queen Elise,* a chilled martini in one hand, a cigar in his other, observing another load of guests as they stepped excitedly from the launch onto his yacht. The ship was already brimming with smartly heeled party goers. Some he recognized from his visit to the UN on behalf of his father. Others were local politicians, journalists and CEOs of businesses interested in opening offices in Elbia. One man was a playwright who currently boasted two hit musicals and a comedy on Broadway. They drank freely of his champagne and nibbled politely from trays of hors d'oeuvres circulated by servers from the sole caterer in Nanticoke.

Not one among the beaming faces that gushed with greetings for him and wished good health for his father, the king, was Alli's. He didn't really expect her to show, but he couldn't stop himself from looking for her.

Over an hour after the party started, the launch appeared yet again. This time it was empty except for its young skipper, in his nautical whites, and a single passenger. Jacob lost interest in the guest's identity once he'd determined the newcomer wasn't wearing the vibrant blue dress he'd bought Alli for the occasion. The launch slowly circled the yacht as Jacob conversed with an eager banker. He was aware of the motor cutting, idling, but paid little attention otherwise.

Mingling with the salt spray, a faint whiff of a familiar perfume caught his attention. He straightened by inches to look more closely at the petite figure climbing the steps into the stern of the *Queen Elise*.

The young woman's hair glittered like spun gold in the late afternoon sunlight. It was brushed out long and smooth, down her back and away from her face. The strands blew delicately in the sea breeze. Piercing her tiny pink earlobes were simple gold knots and clinging interestingly to her body was a silky pantsuit that might have doubled as lounging pajamas. The effect was a mysterious blend of casual elegance.

Intriguingly, the color of her garment so nearly matched her skin, when he observed her from a particular angle and with the setting sun backlighting her—she almost looked as if she was without any clothing at all. It was impossible from a distance to tell where cloth ended and skin began. Only when the air moved around her as she stepped gracefully onto the deck, could he see the outline of sheer sleeves that draped gracefully along her arms and floated on the ocean's breath.

"Welcome aboard!" he called out to her through the crowd of guests, turning away from the banker. He noticed she was carrying a small canvas bag. An overnight satchel? He felt a distinct surge of hope.

Allison shaded her eyes and observed him as he approached her, a small smile playing over her lips.

"You look stunning," he said, aware that most of his guests were watching him and the late arrival very closely.

"Thank you," she said demurely.

"Didn't the dress I bought you fit?"

"I'm not in the habit of accepting gifts from strangers," she said quickly.

It stung. A stranger. Was that how she thought of him? They'd slept in each other's arms, explored each other's bodies intimately. Yet, in honesty, he'd done as much with other women and he thought of them as no more than strangers. Some, he couldn't even recall their names... Why did it hurt that she felt the same about him?

"Maybe we can remedy that situation," he said, flashing her the dazzling but mechanical smile that had begun so many successful seductions. Leaning close to her ear, he whispered, "Most of my guests will be leaving by dark."

"And I will join them," she said succinctly. "I only came to return *this*."

She held out the canvas tote. He peered inside. Scrunched up in a humble ball at its bottom was the expensive dress he'd bought her.

"I'm sorry—I thought you'd be pleased."

"Why?" she asked bluntly. "Why should a woman fall all over herself because you throw an expensive trinket her way?"

He blinked at her, searching for a comeback. He'd sensed this side of her two years ago, but for some reason it hadn't occurred to him that she'd reject a gift now.

"Oh, I see," she said when he failed to find words for his confused thoughts. "It's always worked before, so why not now? Something like that? Well, there's a first time for everything, isn't there?" She swung away from him nonchalantly, gazing around the deck. "Where's the food. I'm starved."

Jacob watched as Allison sauntered across the deck, smiling pleasantly as she greeted a few of his guests on her way toward the hatch that led below, to the galley. She disappeared down the steps. It took several shocked minutes for him to realize what had just happened.

She'd spurned him!

Perhaps he should have skipped right to his usual second gift, a diamond tennis bracelet. But he had a sneaking suspicion she'd have quite literally flung it in his face. What was wrong with the woman? Didn't she appreciate quality?

Gradually, anger crept in over his incredulousness. Every muscle in his body tensed. He felt as if he were standing under a blazing sun, although the air was cooling as a purple dusk wrapped itself around the yacht. Miniature lanterns, strung along the deck rail, flickered on, casting a golden glow across the deck. With a low growl of aggravation, he tucked the canvas tote under his arm and strode toward the steps to the galley.

An elderly couple stood talking with Allison. He cast them a black look; they politely ended the conversation and headed up the steps.

Jacob grabbed Allison's arm, stopping her from reaching for a marinated mussel on a serving tray. "*What* are you trying to pull?"

"Pull?" she asked, innocently.

"Yes, pull. Do you think you can up the ante by giving me back the dress? What is it you want from me?"

She turned her head away, as if pretending to study the array of fresh sliced melon and tropical fruit.

"Look at me, Alli," he ordered.

She ignored him, but he felt her arm lock nervously beneath his fingers.

"Look at me!" he roared.

She twisted free and faced him, her chin lifting defiantly. Her eyes leaped with aquamarine flames. "I'm looking," she pronounced tersely.

"Why did you return my gift?"

"I don't need anyone to buy me clothes."

"I see," he said slowly. "Then I was right. You *are* looking for something more from me." He hadn't expected this of her. It seemed that people did change, after all. "You might as well lay it on the line. What is it you want from me?"

She fixed him with a cold, challenging glare. "Nothing. I want *nothing* from you, Jacob. That's why I came here tonight—to make that point."

"Liar."

Instead of reacting in anger as he'd expected, she took a long moment to coolly study him, her pretty eyes drifting down, then up his tall, trim body. "Why should I lie to you? Has that been your experience with women? They always want something from you?"

"Always," he ground out.

She nibbled her bottom lip contemplatively. "I expect so. But there's a reason for that, you realize."

"What?"

"They expect a payoff, because those are the ground rules you always establish for your relationships."

"What the hell are you talking about?" he shouted. Ground rules? The woman was maddening. He hardly ever raised his voice, but she made him want to bellow like a longshoreman. "I'm very nice to the women in my life. I—"

"I didn't say you weren't nice, in your own material way. What I meant was, you apparently have a reputation for becoming bored with lovers and chucking them out faster than a fashion model changes her shoes. If a woman with any sense at all gets involved with you, she knows she's going to be dumped in a matter of weeks. So she views you the same way you view her. You take what you can from her, and she takes the only thing you're selling—expensive baubles."

Jacob glared at her. "You make me sound pretty damn shallow. I'm not like that. Ask Thomas!"

She laughed and shook her head, sending a smooth blond wave shimmering. "Who's Thomas? Your *manservant?*" Her tone was clearly disparaging.

She was driving him nuts. What right did this small-town librarian have to analyze him? "Well, yes…Thomas is my chauffeur and bodyguard and many other things, but he's also my friend."

"And I'm sure he's generously compensated for taking your side in any discussion," she stated.

He read in her eyes that she understood she'd stepped over some invisible line with her last barb. Doubt flashed across her face.

Jacob felt heat rise in his own. Suddenly, it seemed impossible not to grab her, and he did. He wanted to shake her, shake her hard and make her understand he wasn't a bad man at all—it was just that the world refused to treat him like other men. Things had always been different for him. He was given special privileges, yes. But there were rights other men took for granted—like privacy, choice of education and occupation, the ability to live wherever one wished and marry whomever one chose. He would never have those things.

This time, when he gripped her arm, he let her know through the pressure of his fingers on her flesh that she wouldn't be able to break free until he was ready to let her go. "Thomas never gives less than his honest opinion, even if he knows I won't like it," he growled at her.

"Really," she said. "And what did Thomas say about you and me, two years ago? Or wasn't he part of your royal retinue at the time?"

Jacob winced. She was playing rough. "He was my driver while I was attending undergrad courses at Oxford, in England. After that, he stayed on as my personal assistant, man Friday, chauffeur...whatever I needed. He was also with me when I was at Yale, but I told him I could fend for myself while he took a well-deserved trip home to visit his family in London."

"So he never knew about me?" she asked.

"No." Why did he feel as if he should drop his head and stare ashamedly at his feet whenever she confronted him with their past? It wasn't like him to feel guilty about anything he'd done. But then, he'd never produced a child from one of his affairs, until the one he'd had with Allison. "Look, I didn't force you to become my lover. I didn't seduce you with my fortune, promise you a weekend in the Alps, buy you expensive jewelry...."

"That's right," she said, "because you were clever enough to know those things wouldn't work with me."

"I could have promised you I'd marry you or stay with you forever. I never said I loved you."

"No, you didn't," Allison admitted, her voice sounding painfully hollow. Her eyes dimmed for an instant before flashing up at him. "I didn't say I loved you, either."

The bite of her words took his breath away. Why should it matter? It never had before, with other women.

But for some reason, Allison's bringing up the idea left him feeling destitute—as if something precious had been given to him, then abruptly snatched from his hands. He'd never thought much about love, because he equated being loved with not being alone. And he was never alone. Bevies of people had always hovered around him—caring for his basic needs, answering his questions, fetching whatever he preferred for food, clothing, entertainment.

Before Thomas, there had been nurses, governesses, butlers and maids. His mother had died five years earlier, but in a puzzling way he missed her no more than he missed many of his old teachers. The queen often had been too busy to spend time with him. She'd certainly never told him in words that she loved him. He was an only child, so there had been no siblings to rival him for her affections. Love had, in short, never been an issue for him. He wasn't even sure what it meant.

"Alli," he breathed, still holding her arm. "Why do you have to be so difficult, so combative?"

"Me? I'm not being difficult at all, Prince Jacob." She batted her lashes innocently at him. "I've come to say thank-you very much for the dress, but I don't want or need it. I also want to tell you how much I appreciate your invite to this nifty party of yours. I'm enjoying myself immensely. The food is scrumptious, the wine seems a good year. I'd say I'm being totally agreeable."

Her tongue was firmly embedded in her cheek. She was toying with him. Yet Jacob found it difficult to remain angry with her. He was almost overcome by the scent of her, by the electricity sizzling through the flesh of her slender arm, into his hand. The more controlled and reasonable her behavior, the crazier he felt.

"You want *something*," he roared, looming over her. He felt powerful, yet helpless at the same time. "You aren't *that* different from the others."

Her cool glance rose to meet him. "I suppose I do want

something. I'll tell you what it is," she whispered conspiratorially. "I'd give a king's ransom for a decent ham sandwich right now. This stuff is tasty, but it would take a week of nibbling to satisfy a real appetite."

"Knock it off, Alli. Just tell me what you're after and we can quit playing games. It's the kid, isn't it? You want money for him. Fine. I won't even argue the possibility that he might not be mine. If you need money, I'll make sure you have it. But I don't want a word of this leaked to the press or—" He broke off, silenced by the fury reflected in her features.

"You pompous, spoiled brat," she hissed, attempting to shake him off. "I don't believe I've ever met anyone as self-involved as you, Jacob von Whatever-you-are."

He was astonished by her reaction. "I'm offering you any amount you name for a child I've never seen," he objected. "I can't even be certain he's mine! I think that's pretty damn generous, lady."

"And that's exactly why you're all the things I just called you," she snapped at him. "I don't want your money, Jacob. I want you to go away and leave me and my son alone. The only reason I'm here is to avoid the cost of mailing your damn dress back to you." She wrenched her arm out of his grasp. "Get out of my way. I want to leave now."

He couldn't ignore the determination in her eyes. And he couldn't believe how sure of herself she sounded. Finally, he understood. She was asking for nothing from him but his absence. It was the first time in his life he'd met anyone who honestly had no intention of using him. Power, money, prestige by association, bragging rights for sleeping with him... She asked for none of those things. He didn't know how to deal with her.

So he did what his body had been badgering him to do since she set foot on the *Queen Elise*. He intercepted her before she reached the steps, dragged her into his arms and kissed her possessively on the mouth. The kiss lengthened, softened, grew deliriously heady. Finally, he felt the tension

ease out of her body. Her lips yielded sweetly and trem-
blingly opened to his.

Enfolding her more thoroughly in his arms, Jacob
pressed the length of her body to his. Her high, firm breasts
nestled perfectly into the muscled hollow below his chest.
She wasn't struggling, her mouth was open to him, but she
wasn't kissing him back. That bothered him. He met the
challenge. Teasing her with the tip of his tongue, he waited
until she let out a little whimper and her lips began to
respond, moving in answer to his.

Then the strangest thing happened. It was as if she'd
breathed life into him he hadn't felt in years, not since the
summer they'd spent together. He felt himself grow rigid
with anticipation, felt an energy and potency and driving
pulse no other woman had aroused in him since Alli.

He'd believed his coolness toward women was a product
of his preoccupation with his studies, or with his duties as
state emissary for his father, or with the future when he
would be king and assume the heavy responsibilities of
leading his people. But those pressures hadn't lessened in
past weeks. It was as if Allison Collins had the power to
lift him free and clear of the complexities of his life and
let him feel what it truly meant to be a man. He reveled in
the fiery sensations that a string of perfunctory short-lived
affairs had failed to give him.

"Alli," he breathed raggedly, "I wish to God I could
have stayed with you."

"You made a choice," she murmured between his lips
as her fingers skimmed seductively up his shirtfront, raising
tingles in the short hairs underneath the line of buttons.

"No. There never will be a choice for me. My future
was determined long before I was born."

"Poor little rich prince," she teased. But he could tell
she no longer was trying to hurt him as he'd hurt her when
he walked out of her life.

Her gentle taunting aroused him all the more. He wanted
her with an urgency he'd never before experienced. "I
don't need your pity," he ground out, skimming his lips

up the length of her silky throat. "But I suppose I deserve your scorn. Things got out of hand between us...got too serious...went further than I'd imagined they could." He kissed her lightly along the crest of her shoulder, then groaned with the effort to control himself. "I didn't know how to say goodbye. It had never been a problem before."

Tenderly, she lifted his head away from her shoulder, supporting his strong jaw between her palms. She gazed into his eyes. "Something like this would have worked just fine. 'Goodbye, Jacob. We could have been wonderful together, but we're from two different worlds.'"

She slipped down and out of his arms so quickly he was taken totally by surprise. Her sudden absence stole his breath away. He blinked twice before turning around. She was scampering up the ladder toward the deck.

"Wait!" he cried. He reached for her. She was fast. Before he could capture her delicate ankle, she sprang upward and out of his reach. "Damn! Alli, wait!"

By the time he pulled himself up through the hatch, she was halfway across the deck. Thomas was moving toward her, a concerned look on his usually complacent, moon-like face. Her cheeks were flushed a deep red, and her beige outfit swirled around her agitatedly. Alli's fingers reached for and nervously ticked along the brass rail as she spoke with Thomas. As Jacob approached them he could hear her asking Thomas how soon the launch would return.

"I'll call for it immediately, miss." Thomas cast Jacob a dark, condemning look.

"What?" Jacob gasped. "I didn't do anything to the woman! Ask her, for goodness' sakes!"

Allison pressed her fingertips to her burning cheeks and looked steadfastly out over the waves.

Thomas stepped between them, frowning grimly. "Your Royal Highness, I suggest the lady might prefer to be alone while she waits for her ride to shore."

Jacob couldn't believe it. The two of them were ganging up on him. "I did *nothing* to her!" He peered around Thomas's formidable body at Alli. "Tell him."

She hesitated, as if considering all possible implications of a response. Slowly, she faced Thomas. "The prince didn't hurt me. I'm upset because of…some family news."

The Englishman studied her open expression for a moment before stepping back from between them. "I'll call for the launch," he said in a quiet voice. "I'll be nearby if you need anything, miss."

She nodded, then turned back to observe the water.

Jacob became aware of the guests milling around them on the deck. Most made a point of moving away, aware that something had happened to distress their host. Something dark and dangerous in his expression warned them to stand clear.

He stepped closer to Allison. Her cheeks were returning to their natural pale pink hue. Her fingertips had quieted on the rail.

"You're right," he whispered. "There is no excuse for the way I treated you. I tried to tell you, it has never been difficult for me to break off relationships. Leaving you as I did…it just seemed to fit the mold of what was expected of me." Hadn't old Frederik actually told him, years ago, that brief, dispassionate relationships with women were best? Sex was fine, as long a man protected his heart and his heritage. "I learned to take advantage of…of who I am, I guess."

"What difference does it make, who you are?" Allison asked quietly. "Everyone has feelings. Getting dumped hurts, whether the man you cared for is a pauper or a millionaire."

He shook his head, wishing he could make her understand. "I should never have gotten serious with you. That was my fault, not yours. By law I can only marry a woman of royal lineage."

She looked thoughtfully out over the water, struck through by silver threads of moonlight. "Then, as long as you dated only commoners like me, you had a convenient excuse for ducking out?" she asked.

The word *commoners* sounded so wrong when applied

to her. Allison was anything but a common woman, he thought. "I did date women who came from noble families. But in those cases, the young ladies are educated to…well, not to press, shall we say. They know that when the time comes, I'll be forced to pluck a mate from a very small pool of fish. If they aren't too demanding, their chances will be better."

"Interesting," Allison remarked dryly. "So, when is the big deadline?"

"The end of this year."

Her mouth dropped open. With obvious effort, she closed it firmly. "You're serious about all this stuff, aren't you? This is the way your life is supposed to work. You are allowed to select a bride from a handful of acceptable women and you have to be satisfied with her for the rest of your life?"

"Well, not entirely…" He coughed tactfully into one hand and avoided her eyes.

"What do you mean 'not entirely'?"

He sighed, looking around to see Thomas chatting with some of his guests. No doubt making the necessary apologies for the prince's distraction. "I want to explain all of this to you. It's the least I can do after the way I've treated you. But the details are complex. Can you stay on board for just a short while after the other guests leave?"

"I—I don't know," she said, sounding doubtful. "My sister has the baby. Diane has a long enough day, taking care of a whole tribe of little ones."

"Please call her and ask," he said. *"Please."* The word felt awkward on his tongue. "I really need to talk with you, alone."

She pursed her lips, scowled at the darkening horizon, tapped her polished fingernails nervously on the brass rail. "I don't know if that's wise," she murmured.

He felt them, too—the electric vibrations running between their bodies, warning him that being alone with and close to her might not be wise. But he refused to heed them.

"I won't try anything. I promise, nothing will happen that you don't want to happen, Alli."

She stood silent for a while. When she looked up at him again, he could tell she'd made a decision. "All right. I'll stay, but just until midnight. I'll call Diane."

Allison couldn't believe how difficult the next hour was. She had lost her appetite completely and she found it nearly impossible to carry on an intelligent conversation with anyone. Although she made a point of moving away from Jacob, to put a few feet of desperately needed distance between them, her head cleared only slightly. Whenever she glimpsed his tall frame walking past her, she had to force herself to breathe. She feared she would pass out from lack of oxygen.

At eleven o'clock, she noticed Thomas, circling through the guests, speaking to them quietly, ushering a few at a time toward the launch. Soon those who remained were thanking Jacob for his hospitality and departing.

He was a gracious host, she noticed. But he kept searching her out, as if to reassure himself that she was still on the ship.

At last they were alone—as alone, she suspected, as Jacob ever could be. The crew remained. From what she could see of them as they moved about their various duties, there was a captain, four or five seamen, a cook, plus two cabin attendants. Thomas also was somewhere on board.

"Come up to the bow," Jacob invited her. "The moon is almost full. It's beautiful from up there, and we can talk in private."

She laughed, shaking her head. "Your idea of privacy must be awfully different from mine." Two of the crew were stacking deck chairs, while another gathered used glasses and plates. They looked intent enough on their jobs, but she could sense their curiosity. "Can't we go below and talk? I'm not used to having so many people around."

He looked surprised. "All right," he said slowly. "I

thought you might be afraid I'd attack you as soon as we were out of the public eye."

She shook her head. "I've never been afraid of you, Jacob. Not in that way."

He looked at her quizzically. But she chose not to explain. He held out his hand, and she laid her fingers in his palm. She remembered the way their hands had so often seemed to mesh perfectly, naturally. They'd shared countless walks on the beach. It had felt so right, back then.

Jacob led her down the length of the deck, toward a different set of steps, into a narrow companionway on a lower deck. He slid back a pocket door of polished wood, revealing a private lounge. A long, curving couch of creamy leather followed three walls. In the center of the area was a wet bar and remote controls for an entertainment center. Suspended from the ceiling was a TV screen.

"Champagne?" he asked after she'd selected a corner cushion and snuggled into it, curling her legs beneath her.

"I don't think that's a good idea," she said. "Maybe a cola instead."

He nodded, and after pouring two glasses of soda joined her. He lowered himself to a section a little apart from her, as if he understood she needed space. For a long while they sat in silence, sipping rhythmically at their drinks.

Allison sensed that Jacob was as nervous as she, but she couldn't understand why. After all, what was she to him? Why was he bothering to waste time with a woman who had already told him she wouldn't sleep with him again, wanted nothing from him and intended to keep his secret at no cost to him?

Unless...unless her most terrifying fears were true and he planned to take Cray from her. In that case, she'd rather know his intentions now, because she would fight him to her last breath.

At last, he cleared his throat softly and began to speak. "I believe that your son is my son also—" He held up his hand to stop her from interrupting, when she opened her mouth to protest. "By that I mean it was our making love that created him, nothing more. I would never try to steal him away from you, Allison.''

She choked on the words that erupted unbidden from her lips. ''I couldn't bear that!''

''I understand,'' he said awkwardly, then paused again, as if gathering up words, rejecting others. ''I've never had to do this before,'' he apologized before continuing. ''I don't feel very eloquent at the moment.''

Something vulnerable and boyish about him tugged at her heart. ''It's okay. Just say what you're thinking.'' She gave him a sugary smile, to lighten the moment. ''I can't think any worse of you than I already do.''

Jacob rolled his eyes. ''Exactly.'' He cleared his throat again. ''I've been straight with you. I didn't intend to leave you pregnant, although I did intend to leave you forever. I had no plans for ever coming back here. But you've changed me…inside…in some way I can't explain. Things are confusing now.''

''How are they confusing?'' she asked.

''I don't know,'' he admitted. ''It's as if I'm suddenly trying to live two different lives, because of your…our baby. Before I came back here and saw you and learned I was a father, I took it for granted that I'd eventually marry a suitable woman, although it might not happen as soon as my father would like. And when he stepped down from the throne, I would step up with her at my side. If I ever did fall in love with a woman, which I doubted would ever happen, I'd find a way to keep her close to me while—''

''You mean you'd keep a mistress, in addition to having a wife as your queen?'' The idea appalled her. Yet she knew such arrangements had been made by men of power throughout history. They played by their own rules and the world looked the other way.

''Yes,'' he admitted. ''I would satisfy whatever physical hungers or need for true affection by keeping a lover. My marriage would be purely political.'' He put his empty soda glass on the bar and looked at her as if waiting for her reaction.

Allison met his dark eyes, slowly absorbing what he was trying to tell her in his maddeningly circuitous way. His meaning seized her all of a sudden. She felt a rush of heat through her chest, rising up her throat to her cheeks. "No, Jacob," she whispered. "I could never live that kind of lie."

"It doesn't have to be a lie," he said hastily, as if trying to get all of his thoughts out before she could stop him. "These things are understood in sophisticated circles. We could even travel together. And Cray—that's his name, right?—he would have the very best of everything. You would own a lovely house, in which to raise him, and never have the least worry about money for your own needs or his education. And I'd spend as much time as possible with the two of you and—"

She placed her fingertips over his lips. An overwhelming feeling of sadness engulfed her. She could see a need in Jacob's eyes far more poignant than any he'd expressed in words. He was lonely, although he didn't know it. And he would live out his life without a sincerely loving and faithful companion, because the rules were so different in his world. She felt sorry for him. But she also resented what he was proposing to her.

"I could never live like that," she repeated in a whisper. "I don't care what your sophisticated society allows. What matters to me are the people *I* care about. How would I explain you to Cray as he grew up? Would you be his father? Or should I tell him to call you Uncle Jacob? Now, that's original," she remarked, not bothering to hide her sarcasm. "And what do I tell my parents? Should I explain that I'll never wed because I'm a married man's mistress and intend to live my life meekly, in his shadow? They're sensible, ordinary, good people—who raised me to believe in marriage and fidelity. Two years ago, when you and I were together, I thought—" She let her hand drop from his lips. "Never mind."

He looked at her solemnly. "You assumed we were in love and would get married."

"Yes," she whispered. "But we've been over this, so..."

He reached across the leather cushions to take up her hands in his. Bringing them to his lips, he kissed her fingertips. "I'm sorry, Alli. I'm so sorry. I didn't mean to lead you on or leave you the way I did. I just—"

"I know." She pushed herself to her feet. Everything had been said. What was the use of tearing themselves apart in front of each other. There were no words to make the pain go away. What each of them wanted and needed was totally different. Through the confusing whirl of emotions, that much was clear to her.

"Don't go yet," Jacob grated out the words.

She looked down at him and saw what she most dreaded—a hunger rising in his eyes. Eyes that pulled her into their depths, refusing to release her. She let out a sharp gasp and shook her head. "No, Jacob. Don't—"

He pulled her down on the couch beside him. "Just sit with me for a while longer. The crew...Thomas...they're busy and won't come down here. I've locked the door, just to be sure."

"I can't," she choked out.

But the sound of his voice as he continued to plead with her to stay was hypnotic. His lips, grazing her fingertips, sent ripples of pleasure through her arms. She let her head fall back and her eyes drift shut, remembering how beautifully they'd made love in those gentle summer months. She'd been so happy then.

"I was your first, wasn't I?" he asked. His lips moved seductively up her arm, telegraphing delicious tingles through the sheer fabric.

"Yes." A year...a month...an hour earlier, she would never have admitted it to him, but she felt incapable of denying the truth now.

His moist lips feathered kisses along the curve of her shoulder and circled her throat. "And since then?"

"No one," she whispered throatily. "No one."

"Oh God, Alli." His voice was coarse with passion. "If I could be another man—"

But you can't, she thought sadly. With effort, she forced her eyes open a slit. He was so close she felt the thick heated puffs of his breath between searing kisses that traveled up her chin, reached her lips. She swam in a sea of fiery sensations. The room tilted, spun, dropped away. She felt as if she were floating upward on a volcanic plume—and there was no escape.

But truly, she had no wish to escape Jacob. The realization hit her with a powerful jolt. She wanted everything Jacob was giving her. She had hungered for each touch and sensation assaulting her body and mind. She blocked out of her consciousness everything but this one moment.

His hand moved from the small of her back upward to her nape. He pressed her to him. She didn't struggle. It seemed so long since she last made love. Yet in all that time she'd never wanted anyone but Jacob.

The months of loneliness, the responsibilities of motherhood, her work at the library and simply living through the day-to-day routine of life—all lifted like an enormous weight from her body. There had been happy times, yes. With a baby in the house, how could there not be? But loving her little boy, her parents and her sister's family were far different from sharing the love of a man who was meant to be her partner for life.

That was how she'd thought of Jay—the young man who'd swept her off her feet one sunny day at the beach. She had believed he was her soul mate, in the truest of all ways. But it turned out he was only a fantasy, and this other far more exotic and complex man, Jacob, Prince of Elbia and dedicated playboy, was her reality.

How strange, she thought—it ought to be the other way around.

Reality...fantasy...the two seemed muddled in her mind as she succumbed to the heady potion of Jacob's kisses, which sent her world reeling. With a sigh of surrender,

Allison let Jacob's voice, hands, mouth sweep away all doubt.

Jacob moved with military purpose, quickly unbuttoning the bodice of her pantsuit, letting the cool air of the cabin sweep over her fevered skin, prickling it with beads of sweat. His eyes felt as if they were burning into her very essence, as they locked onto hers. Slowly, his glance trailed from her face down the silky line of her throat, following the vee of her bra. With an expert touch, he flicked open the tiny plastic hook in front. Delicate lace cups fell open and her breasts spilled out, creamy and full, nipples dark and already achingly hard. His breath heated them from hot to scalding. Every sensation felt better than new to her, as though rediscovery of passion brought added intensity and pleasure.

Jacob suddenly stopped moving. She looked up at him, fearing he was going to stop. She found him gazing at her breasts. "You are beautiful...all of you," he whispered. He looked almost embarrassed in that moment. "Did you nurse our son?"

She drew in a sharp breath. The intimacy and implied emotions in the question shook her. "Yes," she said.

He placed his hand over one of her breasts and slid it over the nipple, bringing it to a high, tight bud. "Yes," he repeated, and lowered his mouth where his hand had been and sucked ravenously.

Allison wrapped her arms around his head and pressed him harder to her breasts, delighting in the waves of moist delight the motions of his mouth teased from her.

"Please, Jacob," she groaned down low in her throat. "Please..."

He let her breast slip slowly from between his lips and dropped his head forward, sending a lock of black hair tumbling over his forehead. "It will *kill* me to stop. Been so long—" He broke off with an agonized growl and started to pull away from her.

"No!" she cried. "That's not what I mean!" He'd misunderstood her. "*Don't*...stop. I mean—"

Unable to explain, she showed him by stripping off her remaining clothing. He needed no further invitation. In seconds, he ripped off his own clothes and fell on top of her. Arching her hips against him, she gloried in the rigid proof of his desire for her. "Yes, please, now," she pleaded.

Nothing had changed...no promises were made, no plans spoken, no dreams shared. This moment in time was all she could count on and she knew it, profoundly. She didn't care. A single intimate act became her only consciousness. She trembled as Jacob's lips slid between her breasts, descended over her stomach, stopping to torment her navel, along her abdomen, all the while leaving behind a trail of soft kisses. Finally, she felt his breath center over the pale curls between her thighs.

She draped her long legs over his muscled shoulders, bringing herself closer to him. Her body went rigid with ecstasy as he licked the sensitive, moist flesh between her thighs. Wave upon wave of sweet ecstasy crested over her.

Turning her head, Allison smothered her cries of pleasure in a pillow. "Jacob...oh, Jacob...dear Jacob..." No longer did she have any control over the sounds passing between her lips. No longer were the erotic motions of her body a conscious act. She and this man were locked in the timeless dance of passion, cherished by any woman who had ever loved. Everything she touched, heard, uttered, was instinctive reaction to Jacob alone. She gave herself over to him, holding back nothing.

Through swirls of light and darkness, she felt Jacob settle her hips back into the cushions and shift above her. She opened her eyes. Out of their corners, she glimpsed his bare chest and firm flat belly, glorious with thick black hair, lowering over her. He gently nudged her chin around with one finger and shoved the pillow away so that she had to look into his near ebony eyes. His hand pressed between their bodies for an instant, then she felt his hard tip between her thighs, moving into her. Deeper. Deeper still. Filling her and stretching the taut, unused feminine muscles as he began thrusting.

"You are mine," he chanted in a low, resonating voice. "Mine...mine...mine...my Alli."

And with every possessive syllable he proved his claim by penetrating to her very soul and lacing fiery pleasures with honeyed little bursts of pain. She clung to his sweat-slick shoulders, fearing her heart would burst, knowing only that the world as she'd known it must be coming to an end. And she simply didn't care because oblivion was far, far too delicious.

Four

Jacob opened one eye. He lay on his chest, across a wisp of caramel-colored fabric that Allison had been wearing a few minutes earlier. He could smell her scent among the threads.

Gradually, he became aware of subtle motions beside him. He turned his head, opened the other eye and looked over his shoulder to see her curled up beside his hip. Her arm was lying limply across his back. Her long, pretty legs entwined with his.

It all came back to him in vivid, sensual flashes—like scenes viewed under a strobe light.

"Oh, Lord," he breathed, turning his head away so that she wouldn't see the disgust on his face.

Not disgust with her...with himself, for what he'd just done. He'd nearly destroyed her once, and here he was messing up her life all over again! He had gotten so carried away, he hadn't even reached for the condoms in the drawer beside the couch. Yet he couldn't deny the sheer satisfying pleasure of making love to Allison, or the intensely welcome sense of release that followed his climax. Even now, as he lay next to her—hearing her soft, sated breathing—delightful aftervibrations hummed through his nerves.

It had been a long time since he'd been able to make love to a woman completely. Oh, he'd flirted with, seduced and satisfied plenty of them. The Allison of two years ago wasn't the last woman who'd had trouble resisting the charm he'd nurtured and refined since he was an adolescent, first discovering girls. But after his affair with her, things were different. Sure, he could still go through the motions and fully satisfy his lovers. Few of them realized he left their beds without reaching his own climax. Women might fake it more easily, but a man could find ways, too.

Jacob cursed under his breath. Why was making love with *her* so easy?

He lay still, listening to the rhythm of her breathing, feeling little contented moans that still echoed deep within her chest. He thought he heard her whisper his name, but couldn't be sure. Alternately, her body shivered, then tightened, belatedly reacting to her own shattering climax.

"Sorry," he said bluntly. "That shouldn't have happened." He was at a loss for anything else to say.

Allison seemed to stop breathing at the terse note in his voice.

He pulled himself free, rolled to one side on the leather couch, and sat on its edge, his face buried in his hands. He'd hurt her before, now he'd multiplied the harm tenfold. He hadn't intended that. But it was hard to think of another person's feelings, when all he'd ever known was looking after his own.

Sometimes, he hadn't needed to do more than just think.

Thomas knew his tastes in women. If the prince glanced wistfully across the room toward a pretty female at a party or reception—good old Thomas was on the case. How often had his bodyguard/chauffeur delivered notes, flowers, invitations to young women on his behalf? His friend had rarely disappointed him. The same could be said for the young ladies.

Until Allison entered his life.

Allison Collins was the exception. Jacob had noticed her on the Connecticut beach and was determined to have her. He'd choreographed his approach like a trained dancer planning his own routine.

Of course, after Thomas returned from his holidays he continued filling Jacob's social calendar with beautiful, clever young women. But Jacob hadn't been able to...

Feeling a flush of masculine shame, he shot up off the couch and grabbed something from the floor that resembled the casual pants he'd worn earlier that night. "Get up!" he roared. He pulled on the khakis, not bothering with underwear, and zipped them recklessly.

Allison perched on a cushion that had tumbled halfway onto the floor. She hadn't a stitch on. She was frowning at him, looking puzzled and worried at the same time. "What did you say?"

The aggressive tension in her voice made him instantly wary. He had expected tears, even a pitiful refusal to vacate the ship. He'd prepared himself for female hysteria at its soap opera best. *Why let a few minutes of weeping bother you?* a dark voice inside him demanded. *She survived you before; she will again. You've done what you came to do, haven't you?*

Absolutely. He'd seen Allison again, and he'd possessed her. That's what he had told Thomas he intended to do. Now he could go on with his life. Whatever had blocked him from fully performing in the past had been taken care of and he could resume a carefree existence. If he was fated to take a royal wife and keep a harem of nubile mistresses—hey, how many men would complain about that!

But Allison wasn't crying. And she wasn't flinging objects at him or clinging to him while wailing out her distress. She simply stared at him as if he were a rather large and ugly bug that had dropped unexpectedly from the ceiling.

She moistened her lips and asked again, "What did you say to me just now, Jacob?"

He swallowed and reached down for his shirt, then shook it out. Most of the wrinkles stayed. He dragged it on anyway.

"I said, get up. It's time for you to leave."

"Oh, is it?" she responded, much too calmly.

"Yes. You told me that you had to leave by midnight. Must be after that by now."

"I believe that was before our *discussion* turned physical."

"So?"

"Jacob!" She bit off his name viciously. Her vivid blue-green eyes blazed mockingly at him. "What happened here, just now, wasn't just sex."

He laughed uneasily. "It wasn't?"

"Look at me," she demanded.

He pretended to be busy straightening up the room. He found her panties under an errant pillow and flung them at her. At last her silence and a lack of anything else to do with his hands forced him to face her.

She was hugging a little bundle of clothing in her lap. The sight of her naked breasts made him ache. He fought back the tempting first signs of a returning arousal.

"What?" he barked at her.

"You can't tell me that it's always like this for you."

He held her glance with effort. "How would you know? You weren't there."

"No," she admitted, her tone wavering as if she weren't quite as sure of herself as she pretended. "But I have a sense."

"Well, you're wrong," he snarled, lurching toward her. "Don't read anything more into this than there is. You said yourself, you haven't been with other men. You can hardly claim to be experienced. It's purely physical, sweetheart!"

He could sense the scream swelling in her throat before it exploded between her lips. "Don't you *dare* throw my naïveté in my face!" she shouted, making no effort to contain her voice to the cabin. "Just because I don't romp from bedroom to bedroom across five continents, doesn't mean I don't understand lo—" She blinked at him, either unwilling or unable to finish the last word.

"Love?" he sneered. "Is that what you think this was?"

She sealed her lips and glared defiantly at him.

"That's what you were going to say, wasn't it? You admitted you thought we were in love before. Well, it was a summer fling, just like you said. Nothing more."

"Then why? What was—" She waved her hand at the spot where they'd lain, making love moments before.

He felt his face flush hot and turned away from her. "It was *sex.*"

"Oh," she said, her voice dropping to a whisper. "I see."

He closed his eyes, feeling her pain as if it were his own. But what option did he have other than to push her out of his life?

Jacob swayed from one foot to the other, longing to escape from the cabin where the scent of their passion still clung to the air, luring him back to her. It hurt too much to remain in the cabin with her. He felt desperate to be rid of her and at the same time shameful, cruel and lower than the humblest parasite. Putting space between himself and Alli was the only way he knew to make himself feel better.

"I'll wait topside for you," he said gruffly. "There are towels and soap in the bathroom for washing up, if you like."

Before he'd finished speaking, he was halfway up the steps to the deck.

The caterer had finished clearing away the food and his equipment and was gone. The crew had stacked deck chairs, hosed down tables and deck and turned in for the night. Thomas stood at the stern, smoking a cigar. His mouth closed firmly around the roll of fragrant tobacco leaves between puffs. He seemed to be concentrating on the moon's slender, wavering reflection across the shallow waves.

"Will the young lady require the launch?" Thomas asked, his inflection bleached clean of emotion.

"Yes." Jacob let out on a ragged breath.

Thomas nodded, his expression beneath the dark beard still unreadable. "Strange, she didn't sound particularly pleased with you just now."

"I know."

"Most of them are quite satisfied."

"Right."

"You gave her a parting gift?"

"She wouldn't have taken it if I had."

"Really."

"Yeah, really," Jacob grumbled. Leaning over the gleaming brass rail, he stared down into the cove. The water looked almost black. They might have been floating in the deepest sea. A place without a bottom, without an end to the cold, dangerous depth. "I bought her a dress to wear tonight. Cost more than she could get for her wreck of a car. She wore something of her own, hauled the Givenchy back in a shopping bag."

Something seemed to tickle the corner of Thomas's mouth. His lips lifted slightly. "She's a different sort of girl, isn't she?" He reached for the cell phone on the bracket beneath the rail and spoke into it briefly, then hung up. "The boy will be here with the launch presently, Sir."

Jacob scowled at him, too tired to react to the subtle timbre of disapproval in the man's voice. Jacob's head suddenly felt too heavy to hold up. His stomach felt as if something he'd eaten was curdling there. Allison would leave tonight and he'd never see her again. Even if he begged her to stay, she wouldn't. Not after the way he'd treated her.

"Thomas, there's something you should know," Jacob murmured.

"Yes?" The Englishman blew a lazy blue smoke ring into the night sky.

"She hates me." He didn't wait for his friend's usual

laconic reply. "And she gave birth to a baby almost a year and a half ago. A boy. It's mine."

Jacob waited for his friend's response, for any indication that he thought the situation was ironic, amusing... shocking. At last he turned to observe Thomas's face.

The Englishman tossed his half-smoked cigar into the ocean and met Jacob's eyes. "You are certain the child is yours, Sir." It wasn't even a question. It was a statement, as if he knew.

"Yes. Allison wouldn't lie. She named him Cray. I haven't even seen him, but I believe her."

"You will have to tell the king."

Jacob's mouth dropped open. He closed it after a minute. "Why?"

"The situation is delicate. It could cause problems later on. You said the child was a boy. Legitimate or not, he or his mother might make claims based on your title."

"But the woman doesn't have a drop of royal blood in her—"

"We should check with your father's lawyers. These things are complicated. At any rate, the king must be told." Thomas paused thoughtfully. "He'll be especially anxious to hear of your selection, following this new development."

"My selection?"

"For a wife. Remember, Sir—before the year is out? There is still time for a Christmas wedding. That will suit the von Austerand tradition, will it not?"

"Yes," Jacob murmured vaguely. "Christmas..." Such a joyous season...usually...

He looked up at the irritating rumble of an inboard motor. The launch glided up to the yacht's hull. Almost immediately, Allison burst from the companionway and shot across the deck.

She didn't as much as glance at the two men standing in the stern. Her eyes were bright with fury. Her mouth, devoid of lipstick now, was clamped in an unyielding line. As Jacob watched her descend the ladder, her long straight hair glinted in the moonlight and he felt something vulnerable snap inside him. He turned away, unable to watch her leave.

Allison gazed dully at the clock radio beside her bed. She hadn't bothered to set it the night before; she knew Cray would wake her. Besides, she didn't expect she'd sleep much after leaving the yacht. She hadn't.

She could hear Cray stirring in his crib in the next room. "September twenty-eighth," she murmured. "Tomorrow will be the twenty-ninth. And after that the thirtieth." Thinking in concrete terms of dates and passing time made it easier to face the day after Jacob had left her—for the second time.

A chill breeze lifted the white Cape Cod curtains that framed her window, reminding her that another summer had gone. But the bitter cold filling her bones came from somewhere other than the ocean's sighs or approaching winter. The memory of Jacob's icy glare as he dressed and rushed out of the cabin lingered in her memory, destroying the tender hopes that had filled her with joy in the few minutes just after they'd made love.

He'd done it again. He'd swept her away in a rush of passion. He'd made her believe there was something special and important about their being together. Never again would she be that foolish. From that day on, no man would take her love without earning it. Her pride would allow no less.

Allison threw off the sheets and dragged herself out of bed. She faced the day stoically, making the best of it in an attempt to soothe her ravaged spirit. After considering her options, she telephoned her supervisor at the library and asked for a sick day. She wouldn't hang around the house and feel sorry for herself, though. She would spend the day with Cray. Just her and Cray together for an entire, relaxing day. She took him grocery shopping, then stopped at the department store on the way home and spent money she shouldn't have on a new stroller—the high-tech kind in which she'd seen women joggers pushing their toddlers.

She decided that burning excess energy was a matter of
survival. Perhaps a welcome side effect would be to more
rapidly erase Jacob from her heart.

Later the same day, she dressed Cray in a cozy hooded
sweatshirt and herself in jogging sweats. They ran on the
paved path above the dunes of Nanticoke Cove. The sound
of the waves lapping the sand seemed to call to her. She
couldn't stop herself from looking out over the water. A
dozen pleasure craft bobbed in the marina, but the cove
was empty. The *Queen Elise* was gone.

By the middle of November, Connecticut had seen its
first snowfall. Although only a few inches settled over the
towns skirting the shore—further inland, billowy white
drifts a foot thick covered the hillsides and feathered evergreens and fence rails. One Sunday, Allison talked Diane
into bundling up her three kids and driving north with her
and Cray.

They found a state park and played for two hours in an
unblemished field of the cold, white stuff. Cray toddled in
circles, giggling with delight, repeatedly falling face first
into the snow. The older children pulled him out and
showed him how to make a snowball. When they at last
piled back into the car, they left behind a rare snow creature
with the head of a deer—including antlers fashioned of tree
branches—body of a bear and legs that resembled an ele-
phant's. On the way home they sang nonsense songs and
stopped at a country inn for an afternoon brunch of rasp-
berry hotcakes with maple syrup, Canadian bacon, steaming
coffee for the adults and hot chocolate for the children. The
day was a sunny reminder to Allison, after months of desperate unhappiness, that life could be loving and cheerful.

"Come inside for a while?" Diane asked as Allison
steered the car into her sister's street. "Gary won't be home
for hours. He and the crew are out on a kitchen remodeling
job."

Her husband was a contractor who did everything from
roofs and decks to interior renovations. His hours were long

and they both worked terribly hard, but the marriage seemed a strong one and Allison was glad for her sister. She could imagine a day in the future when all their work and saving would pay off, and the kids would be grown and living on their own. Then they'd have each other. They were good together and would make it.

"Cray's pretty beat. I should take him home and put him down for a real nap."

He had dozed most of the way home in his car seat, but she could probably drop off her sister, nieces and nephew without waking him.

"Lay him down on my bed. We'll send my tribe outside and have a quiet cup of tea. I want to show you the quilt I'm making," Diane added enthusiastically.

Allison didn't have the heart to say no. "Well, okay," she agreed as they drove the last few blocks, following the road around a final curve. Her eyes widened at the sight of a long black limousine parked across the street from Diane's house. "Looks like one of your neighbors has a big night planned."

Diane let out a low whistle. "Gee, limo and all. The Robinsons' daughter is getting married soon. But I didn't think it was this weekend."

"Don't brides usually prefer white cars?"

Diane shrugged. "Maybe they ordered another for the parents."

Allison plucked Cray out of the car seat and helped Diane hustle her kids inside, long enough for everyone to hit the bathrooms and locate dry clothes. Then the older ones were shooed outside while Diane's youngest and Cray were settled down for naps.

Allison returned to the kitchen to put on the teakettle, while Diane ran down to the basement to throw in a load of laundry. She eased off her boots and extra sweater, just as a knock rattled the back door.

"I'll get it!" Allison shouted, chuckling to herself because she was sure it was her nephew Jeffrey, who constantly forgot things.

She swung open the door, but her grin froze on her lips. "What do *you* want?" she asked, her voice colder than the icicles hanging from the roofline above Jacob's head.

He stood on the slab cement step, looking at her standing there with her stocking feet and cold-reddened makeup-free face, as if she were the last person on earth he wanted to see. "May I come in?" he said crisply.

"I don't see why." Allison stood her ground.

"We need to talk."

"We did that. There's nothing more to say."

"It's about your...*our* son."

Allison's blood ran cold. A pain shot through her heart and brought her hands to her chest. *Our son.* The words carried a clear threat.

"He's *mine,*" Allison cried. "Go away!"

She would have slammed the door in his face, but he stepped into the opening, blocking the weathered wooden panel with his broad shoulders. His body seemed to entirely fill the doorway.

Allison heard Diane coming up the steps. When her sister rounded the corner into the kitchen a startled gasp escaped from her lips, but she recovered quickly. "Geez, close the door! It's freezing in here!"

Jacob pushed the rest of the way into the kitchen, despite Allison's attempt to stand in his way. He wore a soft camel hair overcoat that looked like cashmere, dark charcoal trousers, meticulously pressed, and cordovan leather shoes that probably cost more than most TVs. His black hair was combed off of his forehead, emphasizing his eyes. They were the shade of deepest brown polished mahogany. Irresistible. They fixed on her, like twin gun sights. She felt as if she'd been blown away.

Allison glared at Jacob, her hands on her hips, her feet planted defiantly. "Get out of here."

Diane coughed softly. "I guess that answers my next question. Which was, did you invite this gentleman into my kitchen?" She sauntered across the worn tile to her stove. "Still just two hot teas, then."

Jacob took an enormous stride around Allison toward her sister. "I apologize for being so rude, Mrs. Fields. But I had to find Allison, and one of her neighbors told me she'd come here. I've been waiting for several hours." He hesitated only a beat, then held out a gloved hand. "I'm Jacob von Austerand. Maybe Allison has told you about me."

Diane tipped her head to one side and studied the tall, elegant man before shaking his hand. "Yes, she's said a few things about you, Jacob. But I wouldn't want to repeat them." She smiled sweetly.

Jacob flinched. "I'm sorry that the relationship between your sister and myself hasn't been very smooth. Most of it is my fault." He turned abruptly to face Allison. "That's why I'm here."

"Oh?" she said. "I can't wait to hear what you have in mind this time. Your first visit lasted two months. The next time you decided to drop in on Nanticoke, you stayed for...what was it? Three days? Do you have a spare hour or two between flights, Your Royal Highness?"

"Ouch," Diane muttered, rummaging in the cupboard for clean mugs. "Would you two like me to leave the room so you can duke it out in private?"

"No!" Allison and Jacob shouted at the same time.

Jacob sighed. "I think it would be helpful to have a witness in the room. But if you feel uncomfortable, Mrs. Fields, I'll ask my chauffeur to step inside."

Allison stiffened. "There is nothing you can say that I'll find the least bit interesting."

"Even if your son's future is at stake?" Jacob asked tightly.

Allison shot a panicky look at Diane, who was no longer smiling.

"If you've come to threaten my sister," Diane said shortly, "you can haul yourself out of here this minute, mister. You've put her through enough. This may all be fun and games to someone like you. But we're small-town folk, and our families mean a lot to us." Her voice deepened as she became swept up in her own anger. "Cray is

Allison's child. She has no husband. No man has claimed responsibility for him in the seventeen months since he was born. If you think you can waltz in here and make demands—''

"Mrs. Fields, please." Jacob squeezed his gloved hands into fists at his sides, then forced them open again. "I'm not making a threat. I don't want to hurt anyone. But I have a serious problem, and so does Allison—although she doesn't know it yet. We need to discuss a way to work things out."

"My only problem is *you!*" Allison snapped. "If you'd stay out of my life, I'd be fine."

"You weren't exactly *fine* the last time I saw you," Jacob returned. His eyes glowed darkly with meaning she understood too easily.

Allison gasped. How dare he even hint at the things she'd confided to him during their most intimate moments, with Diane in the room!

But her sister only stared blandly at Jacob, as if she'd made up her mind not to be rattled by anything he said.

Allison, though, couldn't help remembering the night on his yacht—how his hands, mouth and body had possessed her so completely. She looked up at Jacob and saw that he was reading her thoughts. Violently, she jerked a chair away from the kitchen table and heaved herself into it. "All right. *Talk.*"

Seeing that their visitor, welcome or not, was going to stay a while, Diane poured three mugs of hot water and plopped tea bags into them. By the time Jacob had removed his gloves and coat, she'd brought the steaming drinks to the table. He draped his overcoat over the back of a chair and sat in it, laying his gloves in his lap. Folding his hands over a flowered plastic placemat, he leaned forward and looked solemnly at Allison.

"I've never seen my son. Is he here with you, now?"

Allison didn't answer.

"He is, then," Jacob said with certainty. "Don't worry,

I'm not about to grab him and run. I promised you before, and it still stands—I would never do that to you.''

Despite her best efforts, tears brimmed in her eyes. The mere thought of losing Cray tore her apart. ''What good are your promises?''

''On second thought, I'll be in the den,'' Diane whispered, starting to stand.

''Sit!'' Jacob ordered.

Diane sat with uncharacteristic meekness, but not without giving him a black look.

He took a deep breath and said in a gentler voice, ''Please stay. I believe your sister will need you in a moment.''

Allison began to tremble. ''What are you going to do?''

''Talk. Just talk, for now,'' Jacob reassured her. He looked around the cozy red-and-white kitchen and seemed to gather some strength from its simple homeyness. ''We have a situation here that must be resolved. Please hear me out.'' He held up a hand when Allison opened her suddenly parched lips. ''You'll get your turn in a moment. You asked what good are my promises?'' Allison answered with a stiff nod. ''Have I ever promised you anything?''

She considered for only a moment. ''No.''

''No,'' he repeated. ''Over two years ago, when we met, I didn't promise that we'd be together forever. I didn't promise that we'd marry. You took those things for granted.''

''And you never promised you'd stay when you came back a few months ago,'' Allison murmured, focusing on her hands as she folded them in her lap in an attempt to quiet their agitated fluttering.

''Right,'' he said. ''I don't make promises... ever...unless I fully intend to keep them.''

Allison swallowed, sensing that he was about to make a point that had the power to change her life.

''I'm about to make you a promise,'' Jacob said tightly. ''I haven't come here without giving this a great deal of thought. I don't take my offer lightly, and neither should you.''

She wedged her hands between her blue-jeaned thighs, but even that didn't still them. ''I don't want to hear your proposition,'' Allison said dully. ''You've already explained your family traditions to me. The men marry for political motives, then take mistresses. Well, my family tradition is a little different.'' She glanced quickly at Diane, whose eyes had grown to twice their normal size. ''We Collins women expect our men to marry us for love and to remain faithful to their vows. I won't be your mistress, Jacob, no matter what benefits you offer—monetary or otherwise. So you might as well leave.''

Diane rose silently from the table and walked around it, stopping beside Allison's chair to rest her hand on her sister's shoulder, as if to prove solidarity in the face of the enemy. For a long moment no one said anything. Then, from the back room, a faint cry broke through the strained silence.

''Is that him?'' Jacob whispered. Allison stiffened. ''Let me see him,'' Jacob begged. ''Please…''

''It won't make any difference,'' Allison insisted. ''I won't be your mistress, and Cray is staying here with me.''

''I told you, I won't try to take him from you,'' Jacob said. His tone and the seriousness with which he looked at her carried the solid weight of truth.

''All right,'' she said hesitantly. ''Since you're leaving anyway…''

''I'll wait out here…by the phone.'' Diane cast the man who had invaded her kitchen a look that promised she wouldn't balk at summoning the police, if necessary.

Reluctantly, Allison led Jacob down the hallway to Diane and Gary's room. In the middle of the queen-size bed, bolstered all around by thick pillows, sat a little boy with brown eyes so dark and luminous they were nearly black. His hair was not quite as dark, chestnut with glints of blond, like his mother's.

Allison turned around, thinking Jacob was right behind

her. But he was lingering in the doorway, his eyes fixed on Cray in wonder as he absently gripped his gloves with both hands. "Oh, Lord..." he breathed. "He's beautiful."

"Yes," she said.

"He's what...seventeen, eighteen months now?"

"About."

"Is he...healthy and happy and... He's all right, isn't he?"

"He's perfect," Allison said. She discovered to her dismay that a small smile was tugging insistently at her lips. She immediately straightened them to a firm line. "You've seen him. Now you can go."

Jacob took a long step into the room. Allison's heart stopped.

"Do you think he'd let me hold him?" Jacob asked.

"He's going through a clingy stage," Allison said. "He'll fuss."

Jacob moved further into the room, toward the bed. "For the record, I wasn't going to ask you to be my mistress," he said to her, although his eyes never left Cray. "I was going to ask you to marry me."

The room spun. Allison's knees transformed to jelly. She wobbled once, then collapsed onto the edge of the bed. Her mouth made awkward motions. Nothing came out.

Jacob moved closer to the bed, as if ready to catch her should she topple off. When she successfully steadied herself, he turned his attention back to his son and began tapping his leather gloves against one palm. Cray's eyes, a moment earlier wary of the stranger's approach, focused with keen interest on the floppy doeskin fingers.

"That was and still is my proposition. I want you to marry me, to be my wife, to come with me to Elbia."

Allison shook her head in denial and disbelief, but words still refused to come. What on earth was the man talking about? She must be imagining this madness—Jacob standing in Diane's bedroom... Cray ogling the big man's fancy gloves... A marriage proposal?

It was a horrid, cruel dream. She'd just have to make herself wake up.

She closed her eyes, then quickly opened them again.

Jacob was still there.

"What are you talking about?" she cried.

Jacob extended one of the gloves toward the bed, just a little. Cray eyed it enviously and began to crawl toward the strange object, ignoring the man holding it. His chubby hand reached out and tugged. Jacob didn't let go, but he smiled as if the strength of his son's grip pleased him.

"What am I talking about?" Jacob repeated. He let Cray have the glove and didn't object when the little boy thrust one of the buff-colored leather fingers into his mouth to sample its flavor. "It's fairly complicated, but it comes down to a matter of both our needs...and Cray's welfare."

Allison stretched across the mattress to pull her son toward her, but Jacob quickly bent down and lifted the child into his arms. Cray was so obsessed with his new toy he seemed unaware he was being held. The thought sent chills down Allison's spine. How easy it had been for Jacob to lure him. Could anyone have done that? Or did the baby sense this tall man in expensive clothes was his father?

"What's best for Cray is that he stay here with me," she stated firmly. "And what's best for me is to stay here in Connecticut, away from you."

"You're assuming that your life will remain unchanged," Jacob said in a soothing voice, as if afraid of startling the child in his arms. "It won't, I'm sorry to say. That's why I had to talk to you today, in person, to explain what has happened."

Allison stood up shakily as Jacob walked across the room, carrying Cray. Her son was now covertly studying the man's face, while pretending to peer inside the glove. His eyes were calm, curious, and showed no evidence of fright. Jacob's hand came up to stroke the back of Cray's small head. A lump swelled in Allison's throat at the sight of father and son, together. Nevertheless, Jacob's words upset her.

"What are you talking about...my life changing?" she demanded.

"I had to tell my father about us," he said.

"You *what?*" she shouted.

"I told the king about our affair and about Cray. He needed to know he had a grandson. I couldn't risk word reaching him by some other means, taking him by surprise. It would have killed him. He's not a well man. And there were political considerations, as well."

"I'm sure he took the news in stride, given family tradition," she quipped. "Mistresses, and all."

"No, he didn't take it in stride, any more than I did when you told me I was a father. It would have been different if I'd already been married and had a child by my royal wife. Then, the heir and line of succession to the throne would have been established without question. But Cray is my first and only child. Even if I marry now, according to my father's legal advisers, Cray might retain rights to the throne."

"Well, you needn't worry about that!" Allison snapped, reaching out to take her baby back from Jacob. "I would never come after your precious little monarchy."

Cray pulled away from her, buried his face in Jacob's lapel and giggled at her attempts to wrest him from the man. He picked today to outgrow clingy, she thought irritably. Great!

Jacob absently touched his lips to the top of the little boy's head. "I understand that. But what happens when Cray comes of age? He'll have a mind of his own. He might decide that claiming his lawful inheritance is only fair. I'm not sure I'd argue with him. And what if something happened to you and he was raised by someone else? You'd have no control over actions another person might take on Cray's behalf."

"Jacob! But this...this," she stammered, "this is insane! Most people don't even know that Elbia exists!"

"The point is, it does exist. And Cray is my heir, which makes him worth a rather large fortune," he said. "But

that's just my half of the problem. You'll be facing a powder keg of a situation if you stay in Nanticoke."

"What are you talking about? Of course, I'm staying."

He looked at her grimly. "Someone has leaked information about you and Cray to the press," he said. "It's not
clear how it happened, but consider it a done deal. We've
been notified by friends in England that the story will appear in tomorrow's London *Times*. Within twenty-four
hours after that, every newspaper in the Western world will
feature an article about the wealthiest royal bachelor in Europe, his librarian mistress from America...and their illegitimate son. You'll be hounded by reporters. Your sister's
and your parents' lives will become a nightmare of fending
off journalists and cameramen. And it won't end after a
few tasteless exposés. Remember how the Kennedy children grew up? Not a birthday party or first day at school
passed without full press coverage. They had no private
lives at all. It will be worse for Cray—because there is
scandal."

"Scandal!" She let out a strangled gasp. "Movie stars
change partners every other month! Why would anyone
care about me and my son?"

"You haven't been listening," he said, moving toward
her so that they were separated only by the few inches
occupied by Cray, still snuggling against his father's chest.
His voice was tight with tension. She could see faint worry
lines across his brow and around his eyes that she'd never
noticed before. "This is juicy stuff as far as the world press
corps is concerned, and they're running thin on gossip these
days. Your family's lives will never be the same. The best
we can do is try to downplay any element that might be
interpreted as scandalous. Tone things down so that the
story will be less interesting to the public."

Allison gazed at Cray with tears in her eyes. He was
sucking contentedly on Jacob's glove, swinging his feet
rhythmically to his own humming sounds. "But how?
What can we do, now that they already know?"

It killed her to think of what her private life might do to

her mom and dad, especially. She imagined pushy reporters hunting down her parents in Florida, in their snug retirement community. They'd supported her during her pregnancy and in her decision to keep her baby. But she knew they'd been hurt by the callous comments of friends, when people learned their daughter was without a husband. This would be a hundred times worse.

"What can I do?" she repeated desperately.

"Tell a harmless white lie," Jacob said.

Cray started wiggling restlessly. Before Allison could take him from his father, Jacob set him on the bed with the pair of gloves. Jacob straightened up and immediately wrapped his strong arms around Allison. She sensed the move wasn't as much to comfort her as to hold her in one place and make sure she listened to the rest of what he had to say.

"How harmless?" she asked skeptically. She had a clear sense of things sliding downhill from bad to worse. Much worse.

"We get legally married tonight. A press release goes out to all major news services, stating that we've been secretly married for three years. We chose not to make the marriage public because you weren't a royal and there was initially some dissension in my family about that."

"Oh, right. Like people will believe, the way you've been bedding down anything in a skirt, that you have an American wife. No woman in *this* country would stand for that kind of behavior!" she huffed.

"You'll be surprised what people will believe," he assured her. "We can simply say my so-called affairs in the past few years were part of an act. The important thing is, a secret marriage is tantalizing enough to hold the press's interest for a while. There will be a flurry of coverage, interviews and such. But it can be handled very routinely. The palace has press secretaries working on it right now. When anyone in your family is approached, all they have to say is that they are pleased the word is finally out and refer any questions to the palace."

"The palace," Allison repeated. "Do you realize how absurd this sounds?"

His expression darkened; his eyes bored into her. "Believe me, you'll be happier dealing with absurdity than with the notoriety that comes with being labeled the mother of a prince's bastard son. We either take preemptive measures," he said seriously, "or you and your entire family will learn what it's like to play the fox to the gossip magazines' hounds."

"But—" she started to object, grasping at any alternative "—I could take Cray away. I could hide somewhere until things cooled down."

He shook his head and his arms tightened around her, trapping her next to his chest or protecting her there...she wasn't sure which. His heart beat against hers, creating a complex counterpoint rhythm that was strangely soothing.

"Listen, Alli, I've lived all my life with reporters watching me through telephoto lenses and binoculars, picking up on the least little thing I did, waiting for me to take a wrong step. Well, I finally did it. I ran into a woman who made me forget about protecting myself. I got her pregnant, and now we have a son to shelter from this madness." He looked at Cray, and the ebony gleam of his eyes lightened briefly with a touch of joy. "Marriage legitimizes our son and it makes us an almost ordinary couple. TV and newspapers can only make so much of a story like that. They'll run a couple of stories, then grow bored with us and find juicier territory."

As odd as it all sounded, Allison understood his reasoning. The logic was unarguable. But she blushed at the thought of Jacob sitting across a table from his father and a dozen political advisers, discussing their love affair and its disastrous consequences.

"I don't know..." she murmured, studying Jacob's handsome face, reaching up to trace his mouth with her finger without thinking about what she was doing. Was he even now telling her lies? Would listening to him put Cray and the rest of her family in an even worse position? She snatched away her finger. "I hate you for ruining my life. How can I marry you, for any reason?"

"You have every right to hate me," he said stiffly. "Since we're being honest, I resent the hell out of you, too."

Allison pulled back from him as far as he'd allow. "You resent *me?* Why should you, when I didn't do anything to you?"

"Oh, you did plenty, lady." Jacob glared at her. "That summer, I was totally mesmerized by you, Alli. There was nothing I wouldn't have done for you. I stopped being who I'd been all of my life. Suddenly, I stopped thinking about the future. I forgot about all the obligations, all the political planning and social responsibilities." His eyes shifted to the bed. "And we made a baby."

"Yes, we did," she said softly, tears clinging to her eyelashes.

"Now we have to deal with that reality. The methods we're forced to use may not be to either of our tastes, but we don't have much choice."

Allison drew a ragged breath that felt as if she were inhaling razor blades. "Does this mean that Cray will someday be..." She couldn't say *king*. "Will take your place, as you will take your father's?"

"No, the cabinet and my father's advisers are working that out. Because his mother is a commoner, he's not guaranteed the right of succession. His position is contestable. There are a lot of complicated legal twists and turns to be worked out. But the plan, briefly, is for the two of us to divorce after a decent period of time—about a year—and then I'll remarry." His eyes locked with hers, pulling them into his, as if watching for her most subtle reactions. "You won't have to stay married for long to the man you hate."

"I see..." she said calmly, although his words hurt. Of course, she hated him, but why did he have to make it sound as if she had done something wrong by admitting it? "So you and your father's advisers will work out everything, nice and tidy."

He released her and stepped away, his expression now unreadable, a mask of self-control. "This is best for everyone. Not just for my family. For yours, too."

She felt numb with disbelief, but too emotionally drained to argue any longer. "All right," she whispered. "We'll do this your way."

Five

The limousine pulled away from the house. Jacob slumped in the deep seat farthest to the rear in the luxury vehicle. "It's done," he said with a sigh. "She's agreed and I waited while she made the necessary phone calls."

The sharp-eyed older man who shared the spacious passenger area gave a satisfied nod. "A shame it had to come to this," he said crisply in German. "Unfortunately, there's no other way, for the time being, but to marry the woman."

Jacob cringed at the cold analysis from Frederik, his father's most-trusted adviser. Glancing up, he caught Thomas watching them from the driver's seat, in the rearview mirror. His friend had no official involvement in the emergency cabinet meetings that had been called in Elbia the day before. But in those frantic hours since the palace had become aware of the *Times* story, Thomas had found plenty to say in private.

At first, Jacob had intended to simply fly Allison and their son to Elbia, believing he could protect them from stalking journalists if he just kept them close to him and out of sight. But the king's advisers had foreseen problems in keeping a mistress and an illegitimate son inside the country while Jacob continued wife shopping. Thomas had been the one to come up with the idea for an arranged short-term marriage. Frederik and the king had preferred the prince deny ever having known the American woman, but Jacob refused to turn his back on the child and his mother. After heated debate, everyone had agreed that Thomas's plan was the least objectionable course of action.

Jacob hated the idea of forcing Alli to live a lie. In the end, he decided to go along with the ruse only because it was the one way he could save Alli, little Cray and Alli's entire family from humiliation. But as he had flown across the Atlantic to face the woman who had made more of an impact on his life than any other, he found the decision pleased him on another very personal level: at least for as long as he and Alli were legally married, he'd have an excuse to be around her and the little boy who'd so innocently and thoroughly charmed him.

Jacob had insisted on one point, though. Although Frederik traveled with him to meet with Allison, in case a negotiator was needed, Jacob had insisted on first meeting with Allison alone.

Now that he had her cooperation, they were supposed to move on to the next step. The limo was headed for nearby JFK airport, where Frederik would board the Concorde for the return flight to Paris. Jacob would then return to Nanticoke and whisk Allison off to the chambers of an old friend of his father, a New York City judge. After the ceremony, they'd have to watch every word they uttered to friends and strangers alike, and carefully orchestrate their every move—if they were to avoid raising the suspicion of the press.

"*Keine Sorge,* Your Highness," Frederik said soothingly, patting the younger man on the knee with his wrinkled hand. "Don't worry. It won't be so very bad. A year or two from now…no one will remember the woman." The man's accent was thick and leaden, compared to Jacob's, which was almost nonexistent after years of schooling in America and England. Frederik's W's all sounded like V's, and the emphasis often came at the wrong part of the word when he spoke in English.

Jacob cringed at the thought...no one will remember her. Was that really true?

"The wedding, it will be quick and quiet," Frederik continued. "A civil ceremony of no importance. It is all arranged."

Jacob looked up, startled. "How did you arrange it? Until minutes ago, Allison hadn't agreed to go through with the marriage."

The old man cackled. "For a fellow who has had so much experience with women, Jacob, you sometimes amaze me with your gullibility. What woman would turn down such an offer? The money is beyond imagination to a simple American working girl. Her settlement after the divorce will support her and the child in lavishness for the rest of their lives." Crafty yellow eyes peered at Jacob, making him feel uncomfortable.

Frederik knew him too well. Since Jacob had spoken with Allison, thoughts had begun flitting through his mind he'd rather no one know about, until he was ready to reveal them. He turned away from the older man to look out the window of the speeding limousine, shielding his expression from view.

"You did tell her about the money?" Frederik asked in German.

Jacob exhaled slowly. *"Nein."*

A heavy gray brow lifted. "Good God—why not, my boy?"

"I had to know if she'd accept my offer without a bribe," Jacob snapped, furious at being interrogated. "You probably wouldn't understand. I'm not sure, myself, why it matters, but it does." He raked stiff fingers through his hair.

In fact, why should it make any difference at all? They'd boxed Allison in well enough. What choice did she really have but to agree to the plan? She would have had to sacrifice the privacy of her entire family and subject her son to ruthless busybodies, pushy reporters and photographers who would stop at nothing to get a shot of her walking her son to school or stepping out of the ocean in a bikini. Diana, Fergie and even Princess Stephanie of Monaco—all women he'd known for years—had been subjected to countless such invasions. It would be no different for Alli.

But for some reason, not mentioning the money to her made him feel better. It was as if, in some inscrutable way, she had accepted him for himself.

"No matter," the old man said with a dismissing wave of his hand. "The important thing is, the situation is now under control. We have cooperation from American State Department officials to provide necessary documentation for a three-year-old marriage. Even if the press decides to dig, they will find nothing. What about the woman's family?"

Jacob sighed. "They have been instructed by Allison to make no comment about the date or details of our marriage. I stood beside her while she told her sister and telephoned her parents. Her friends were in the dark about the father of the child, anyway; she never told anyone who it was. So they have nothing to say to the contrary."

"Good...very good." The king's adviser chuckled and slapped his thigh, as Thomas maneuvered the elegant stretch limo toward the exit for the airport.

"You don't have to be so cheerful," Jacob grumbled.

"Why not? All is working out quite smoothly. By this time next year, we will have filed the divorce decree. Then you will be free to marry the Contessa di Taranto. Her father is most enthusiastic about the match, even with this minor setback."

"I'll bet he is," Jason sneered, "the greedy old coot."

"The contessa is a beautiful woman. Fertile, I'm told."

"Good Lord, they've checked her out? Like some prize sow!"

Frederik briefly lifted his fingers to cover a smile. He leaned back against the smooth leather upholstery, lit a long brown cigarette between thin brown lips, and puffed with obvious pleasure. "Why leave something like that to chance, dear boy? We are talking of being practical, are we not? We are talking about safeguarding a dynasty. That's why you must legally marry the American woman, then legally divorce her and settle equitably with her."

"You've thought of everything, Frederik," Jacob growled.

The old man arched one brow. "For your father's sake and yours, I hope so. There must be no question as to your rightful heir when you and the contessa produce your real family. By taking these measures now, you will have done the American woman a good turn, saving her family embarrassment and handing her a fortune. To show her appreciation, she will sign papers surrendering the child's future rights to the throne."

A wave of anger and disgust swelled inside Jacob, but he didn't let it show as the car slid along the highway ramp almost soundlessly—an ebony streak among a dusty herd of commuters in economy cars. Now he could only do what was best for Allison and for his country. But he had some ideas of his own for the future. Risky, possibly dangerous ideas. Only time would tell if he could pull off the plan that was even now taking shape in his churning mind.

Snowflakes drifted down from a winter gray sky across Allison's living-room window, later that same day. Across the street, one of her neighbors was stringing Christmas lights along the line of his roof. Jacob felt restless, impatient to do all that had to be done. Nervous prickles danced up his spine. The solid weight of doubt filled his stomach.

"I'm ready," a cool voice stated from behind him.

Jacob turned to face Allison. She wore a pale pink sweater dress with a high rolled collar and long sleeves that snugly enclosed her slim arms. The hem fell sedately to midcalf length. The only jewelry she wore was a pair of simple gold-toned hoops that glittered against the seductive line of her white neck. Her blond hair was brushed back from her face and fell past her shoulders in an uninterrupted flow of brilliance, to the small of her back.

Cinderella, he thought. She looks like a fairy-tale princess, without the fake glitter and pompous airs. Jacob stepped forward, reaching out, and would have pulled her into his arms and kissed her, but she skittered away with a frightened look on her face.

"Jacob, no." His name escaped her lips on a ragged breath. "This is hard enough, as it is. Don't add to my confusion, please."

His hands dropped helplessly to his sides. His heart quaked, shattered in his chest. "Sorry. You just look so...so..." He wanted to say *beautiful*. But he was afraid she'd think he was patronizing her.

"I hope this is all right." She pivoted nervously on two-inch heels. "I wasn't supposed to wear white, was I?"

"No. We're supposed to be on our second honeymoon."

"Yes, you did explain all that before, didn't you," she murmured vaguely, looking off into a mysterious middle distance he wished he could see. Maybe there he'd find answers to how he was going to make everything work the way he wanted, without destroying them both. "Is it time to leave?" she asked.

"If you're ready. You left Cray at your sister's house?"

She nodded. "Diane will keep him until tomorrow night when we come back." She glanced bleakly at Jacob out of the corners of her gentle sea-hued eyes.

Today, most of the blue seemed to have washed away and they were predominantly green. He wished with all his heart he didn't have to put her through this.

"Where exactly will the ceremony be?"

"A judge's office in Manhattan. Everything's been arranged by your State Department. The judge is an old friend of my father's."

"How convenient."

He was relieved to hear a touch of sarcasm in her tone, a signal that her old pluck and combativeness were returning. With them came a healthier pink to her cheeks.

"We'll spend the night at a suite my family keeps on Park Avenue. If all goes as planned, in the morning, before we leave the city, we can see some of the sights...if you like."

Allison frowned at him. "What about reporters?"

"They're never far away from anyone the public considers a celebrity. You'll get used to them. The trick, for us, will be giving them only the information we want them to have." He paused, thinking. "They haven't been trailing me around Nanticoke because they haven't smelled a story yet. Tomorrow, after the *Times* article comes out, everything will be different."

"What do I say to them if they start asking me questions?" she asked.

"Don't worry, we'll rehearse some clever repartee on our drive into the city. We're taking your car, by the way."

"What? No limo?" she teased, her eyes flashing at him mischievously. "However will we survive?"

"No limo, this trip. The less attention we attract until we have a marriage certificate in hand, the better."

Allison insisted on driving. Her little American-bred sedan had been faithful to her for ten years of hard driving, but the deadly combination of winter road salt and blowing sand was slowly rusting out its bottom and its inner works had recently become temperamental. She knew just when to give it another drop or two of gas and how long to ride the clutch to get it to do what she wanted, without stalling.

She took the ramp onto I-95 and headed west toward New York City. They drove for twenty miles or more without either of them saying a word. She sensed a hidden tension gripping Jacob, beside her in the passenger seat. He stared fixedly out the side window at the passing snow-covered landscape. Every now and then, houses came into view, gaily decorated for the holidays with evergreen wreaths, plastic Santas and reindeer, nativity scenes—although Thanksgiving had only just passed.

She felt hopeless, numb, incapable of making important

decisions, as if she'd just been diagnosed with a terminal disease and her days were numbered.

Two years ago when Jacob had left her, Allison believed her life had come to an end. But she'd survived and grown stronger for the experience. Then he'd come back for a mere handful of days, but left for another two months. This time, they would live together as man and wife—for how long she didn't know. But he'd leave her as he had before. She was certain of that much, if nothing else. She didn't know how, but she'd have to find a way to protect herself from caring too deeply for him.

"You promised we'd rehearse my lines," she said abruptly, unable to stand the silence or her own troubled thoughts any longer. "I've been thinking. A librarian sounds too tame. How about I tell the press I'm an exotic dancer and you met me at bachelor's party?"

Jacob turned his head and observed her, his eyes a dense, shadowy ebony. It felt as if they were stripping her bare. Her cheeks blazed under his scrutiny.

"Yes," he agreed looking away again. "At the very least, we're going to have to teach you to lie without blushing."

It was late afternoon, nearly dusk, by the time they pulled up in front of the stunningly ostentatious complex of designer shops and hotel facilities. A valet opened the car door for Allison, pretending not to notice that she wasn't driving a Jag or Porsche.

For the next two hours, the world seemed to function without need of her attention. She felt as if she were being carried along by events. They were whisked skyward in a private elevator to the penthouse suite. Jacob took her arm and strolled her through rooms full of rich furnishings. Waterford crystal tumblers and wine stems sat on a well-stocked bar built into one wall of the central room. Tapestries that looked as if they'd been brought from a castle, hung from the opposite wall. The suite was almost too full of treasures for her to absorb any single one.

Allison allowed Jacob to settle her on a formal couch that looked like something Marie Antoinette might have approved. She sat very still, trying to breathe. She was vaguely aware of Jacob, moving about the rooms, picking up a phone and speaking solemnly into it. Then he was ushering her out the door again and into a cab that rushed them off—as speedily as any vehicle could rush in midtown traffic—to an office not far from the United Nations complex.

There, a man Jacob called Resnicek read off a list of strange questions to Allison. She answered them with as much comprehension as Cray had of astrophysics. The judge's entire purpose seemed to be to reassure himself that she wasn't being forced into signing the marriage agreement against her will. His anxiously protective attitude made her even more nervous than she already was. It seemed to her that this man of law might be aware of issues, dangers, forces threatening her, that she couldn't see.

But what choice do I have? she asked herself, as a lump the size of a pillow grew in her throat. Her hands sweat profusely. Her mouth and throat felt as dry as if she'd been without water for days. If she didn't do as Jacob said, she'd jeopardize her entire family's future. And she would destroy her son's life.

At last, Jacob shouted something at the man in German. The judge shrugged and laid a document on the desk in front of Allison.

"Sign here," he said woodenly. "And initial here…and here."

With a trembling hand, she formed the letters of her name on the lines he indicated. The pen felt like ice in her fingers…or maybe it was her fingers that were so very cold. Then Jacob endorsed the same paper with a hasty flourish. Resnicek called in a secretary, and they both witnessed the signatures. It was done. The whole process was more like taking a written driver's test than getting married, she thought numbly.

But legally—for how long she didn't know—Allison

Collins of Nanticoke, Connecticut was a royal princess.
Wife of the Crown Prince of Elbia.

How they got from the judge's chamber back to their
suite, she had no idea. Details such as walking, the cab
ride, greeting the concierge in the hotel lobby, which
boasted a hundred-foot waterfall and tropical jungle at its
center...they all blurred together.

She found herself sitting stiffly on the edge of a king-
size bed, staring blankly around the room, still wearing her
traveling clothes. There were two other bedrooms opening
into the spacious central room which appeared designed for
business meetings and social receptions. She'd never seen
so many flowers in one place. Urns brimming with roses,
snapdragons, gladioli and mums filled every corner. A long
glass wall revealed a breathtaking view of the New York
skyline against a winter sky. She didn't want to know what
the suite cost per day. She had a feeling the figure would
make her feel physically ill.

Even more ill than she already felt.

Allison stared at her hands, folded in her lap, trying to
grasp at anything that seemed real. A slippery if not impossible venture, it seemed, whenever Jacob entered her
life. She heard footsteps approaching and looked up.

Jacob stood before her. His conservative striped tie was
gone. The collar of his white silk shirt lay open, and he'd
undone the buttons. He wore no T-shirt to cover the dark
curls of masculine hair shadowing his deeply defined chest.
His stomach was flat, ridged with muscle. A subtle tremor
coursed through her. He looked wonderful, and she had to
close her eyes to stop all the wrong feelings from intensi-
fying.

"Are you all right?" he asked, his voice rough with an
emotion Alli couldn't define.

"Yes. I think." She forced herself to meet his dark eyes.
Clearing her throat, she separated her clenched hands and
pressed them flat over the bedspread on either side of her
hips. "What happens next?"

"I suppose you'd better put this on," Jacob said. He held

up a gold ring—a diamond solitaire as big as her thumbnail, centered between two brilliant sapphires.

An involuntary gasp slipped between her lips before she covered it with a forced laugh. "You can't be serious. That's not real, is it? Please tell me it isn't."

"It's real," he said solemnly. "The ring has been in my family for five generations."

The smile dropped from her lips. "I'm sorry, I didn't mean to offend you. Where does a person buy a diamond that big?"

"I'm not sure," he said, studying the jewel. "I've never had to purchase one. This was my mother's engagement ring. Before that, it had been my grandmother's. I believe it originally was among the Russian crown jewels, before the Bolshevik revolution. The center stone is called the Heart's Ember. If you look at the diamond closely, there are flame-colored highlights in it. Like pink fire between the blue of the sapphires." He stepped toward her, holding out the ring.

"I never met a stone with a name before." Gingerly, she plucked the ring from Jacob's fingers. In the instant hers touched his, it was as if a video replay of their night on the yacht flashed before her. Vivid. Hot. Erotic... humiliating. Her hand snapped back, as if he'd burnt her.

He frowned, looking puzzled.

She tried to focus on the ring and come up with something princessy and witty to say. Nothing.

"Wouldn't you rather h-hold onto that for the real princess?" she asked, her voice cracking. "I mean, won't tradition be destroyed if a commoner wears your family's jewels?"

"I think of you as anything but common," he said.

Allison swallowed and gazed up at him, questioningly. Was he just trying to make her feel better? "The whole world will find out who I am in the next twenty-four hours, if what you've said is true, Jacob. There's no way I'll be seen as anything but a small-town librarian, with nothing to call her own but a baby and a beach house." She managed to look him in the eye, to make sure he understood how she felt. "They'll say I'm after your money."

"Doesn't matter what anyone says," he responded gruffly.

She took a deep breath. But it does matter, she thought sadly. If it didn't, he wouldn't be here now, taking part in this charade.

"Any other questions before you put this ring on?" he asked, taking another step toward her.

"When will the lawyers start working on the divorce papers?"

Jacob flinched as if she'd struck him. "Immediately, I suppose. But they won't expect us to actually split up for about a year. Less than that might result in another difficult public relations problem."

She nodded, closed her eyes briefly and let the terrible truth of his words sink in. Then she shook her head.

"What's wrong?" he asked. "That's the arrangement we agreed to."

"It's not a matter of the time," she said, telling only half the truth. "I was just thinking about…about that." She pointed at the ring. "I can't wear something that outrageously expensive. It's not right."

"Give me your hand," he said.

She didn't move.

"Give it to me!" he shouted testily, then reached out and captured her left hand before she could shelter it behind her back.

He slipped the diamond onto her fourth finger. It felt heavy resting there, as if it carried the weight of far more than gold and three stones. Duty, tradition, maybe even the blood of a Romanov who had died wearing it. The ring blazed on her finger.

"It's beautiful," she murmured, not wanting to admit to him how much it frightened her, even as she felt dazzled by it. "But I have no right to it." She started to take it off.

His wide hand shot out and locked around hers. "No!"

he said sharply. "Don't. The ring belongs where it is. I want people to see you wearing it."

"Part of the show?" If she sounded bitter, she couldn't help it. "A ring this huge is like this suite...a foolish waste of money."

He scowled at her, looking as if he was on the verge of losing what little patience remained to him. One corner of his mouth twitched in barely controlled anger.

She had to keep talking, had to throw out objections to make him understand how wrong they were for each other...so that she'd understand, too, and not allow herself to be pulled deeper into the fantasy he was weaving around her. She didn't dare allow herself to start feeling comfortable in his world.

"Imagine how many hungry children this might feed...how many sick people might be given medicine for the price of this bauble," she blurted out the words, pulling her hand free to wave the ring in his face. "Maybe you're not used to hearing that sort of thing. Maybe it's not very sophisticated to scoff at precious jewels or refuse to wear animal fur or think about how many homeless people could be put up in a shelter on a cold December night with what it cost for just one of these stones. But I find it disgusting."

"Are you finished?" he asked tightly, after she'd finally run out of breath.

She gave a curt nod.

"Now that you've thoroughly insulted my family as well as me, personally, I'll have my say."

He moved over her. Bending at his waist, he braced his hands on either side of her thighs, trapping her hands beneath his. His powerfully angled face closed to inches from hers. His eyes burned into hers with a fervor that frightened her.

"Someday I will explain to you the importance of jewels and titles in today's world. But for now, Princess Allison, you *will* wear my ring and you will flash it in the eyes of every person you meet, no matter how distasteful being my wife may be to you. I need the world quickly convinced that our marriage is real." He brushed his lips over hers, but she held hers taut, unyielding. When he pulled back, the anger in his eyes had turned brittle, cold, terrifying. She wasn't sure which was worse—the black flame or the dark ice. "Is that understood?" he ground out.

"Yes," she whispered.

It suddenly occurred to her that if she failed to keep her end of the bargain and effectively play her role in this matrimonial deceit, Jacob would very probably feel no obligation to keep his part of the deal—which was to allow her to keep Cray. The fear must have shown in her expression, because something changed in the way Jacob was looking at her. The fury in his eyes moved aside, like a smoothly sliding door, revealing layers of other emotions—concern, need, his own set of fears...and unmistakably, lust.

She moistened her lips and moved them stiffly until they made words. "You think I'm insane, don't you?" she whispered, hoping she could sidetrack him. "I should be jumping up and down and screeching with delight at my good fortune. This ring..." She held up her hand. "It *is* exquisite, Jacob. I don't mean to belittle it or your family's traditions. I'm sure they both mean a lot more to you than the price a jewel would bring at Christie's. I'm sorry, I can't help it sometimes. Money seems such a necessary evil. We all need it to survive—but too much of it makes me nervous."

"You're sexy as hell," he rumbled from deep within his chest. His eyes seemed to fill up with her reflection.

So much for sidetracking, Allison thought. She tried to extricate her hands from beneath his. He allowed them their freedom, but quickly pulled her to his chest.

"What sort of man are you?" she protested. "I've just insulted your ancestors and rejected everything you stand for. That turns you on?"

"No," he said, coaxing her chin around so that he could look into her eyes again. "*You* turn me on. Any other woman I've ever known would be jabbering on, about how she was going to spend her new husband's fortune—

weekend flights to shop in Paris, collecting Fabergé eggs, auctions in London, luncheons in Rome. You act as if having anything over a hundred bucks in your pocket will burn you. You do realize, don't you, that Elbian princesses, by law, are entitled to generous monthly personal allowances from the court. In your case, it's around twenty thousand dollars, in American currency."

She stared at him.

He chuckled. "Bet that blows your pretty penny-pinching mind. Of course, all of your living expenses are already covered, as are Cray's. That allowance is for clothing, travel that's not related to your duties for the palace, personal gifts for friends and family...."

Allison was pretty sure she'd stopped breathing.

"Do you intend to give it all away to soothe your conscience?" he asked, a small smile easing the line of his lips. He was toying with her.

"Well, not *all* of it," she amended, struggling within his arms with less energy. His eyes were really amazing. Intoxicating. "My mom and dad could use a new roof on their house in Florida. But it might be fun to have a new dress or two—something that didn't come off a department store markdown rack."

"Good," he murmured. His lips brushed hers again, then moved lower.

She squeezed her eyes shut and tensed. "Please, Jacob. I can't...I don't want to..."

"I don't want to, either," he said. "But this isn't something either of us can control, it seems. When you're alone with me, it's as if we are parts of a whole, and just happen to be separated by too much air. I have to get closer to you, until there's nothing between us."

Tears worked their way into her eyes. "Don't say things like that."

"Why not?"

"Because—" She couldn't let him know all that was in her heart. He would find ways to use her vulnerability.

Hadn't he left her before, as soon as he realized she was falling in love with him?

"Because," he guessed, "you think I've said these things to other women I've slept with?"

Close enough. She nodded, unable to speak over the raw spot in her throat.

"I've never told another woman what I've just said to you. And I've never told a woman I loved her."

She studied the solemn depths of his eyes. "You never said that you loved me."

"I know." The irises of Jacob's eyes dilated, swallowing up the pinpoint black pupils. He locked his arms firmly around her waist. "I won't say those words to any woman until I'm sure they are true, until I'm certain she feels the same way about me, too."

"What if that time never comes?"

"At least I'll know I haven't misled anyone," he said in a voice so quiet the sounds of the city beyond the room nearly drowned out his words. "I've never lied to get a woman into bed. I've never lied to you, Alli—I just didn't tell you everything there was to know about me."

"Which was as good as a lie," she insisted.

"No. A lie is different. A lie robs your soul." His fingers trailed up and down her spine, feathering across her shoulder blades, coaxing her to relax in his arms. "I won't lie to you, Alli. I just can't tell you everything, yet."

"Still?" she asked incredulously. "You're still keeping secrets?"

"Yes, I have secrets. Not just from you. Someday I hope things will be different. But for now I have to keep my own counsel, and you must trust me to keep the promises I do make to you."

"Trust you?" She stared at him. How could he so quickly forget their rocky history? "You've deserted me and our child—twice—and you expect me to trust you?"

He winced. She could almost enjoy the hint of pain in his expression. "I do—but mostly because you have no choice. You need me."

"I don't!" she said defiantly.

He shook his head at her, then kissed her again softly, seductively. "We've been over this. You know that's not true." His lips met hers again, briefly. "Wear my ring. Be my wife," he whispered.

"Jacob, I..." It was so hard to concentrate on behaving sensibly when he was doing such lovely things to her with his mouth and hands.

"I want you, Alli. I want you more than I've wanted any other woman, ever. So help me God, that's the truth."

She brought her hands up between them and framed his lightly whiskered face with her palms. Closely she studied his strong features, his fascinating eyes. "That definitely sounds like a bald attempt at seduction."

"It's not," he said quickly.

Allison smiled at the little boy feistiness in his tone. "How do you expect me to believe a man with a reputation like yours?" she asked, feeling less afraid now. "Diane showed me magazines...photos..."

"Me and my old flames?" His eyes lit up roguishly. "I can't deny having been with some remarkable women. But none could shine a light on you, my sweet Alli. Not one of them has your soul, your generosity, your sweetness...."

Jacob's hands moved around her back, slipping beneath her arms. His thumbs caressed the sides of her breasts through the knit fabric of her dress, as his moist, masculine mouth lowered over hers. She felt she was losing herself completely in his heat, wilting like a flower that had been set under a blazing sun without benefit of water. Lost, she thought distantly, I'm lost.

Six

This is your wedding night, a voice whispered through her mind. This is the night you've dreamt of...and now it's come, and it's all wrong.

Sitting on the bed in Jacob's arms, Allison swayed weakly. Again, the voice echoed maddeningly through her head. His hands moved over her body, and she felt powerless to stop him...didn't want to stop him, for everything he was doing felt wonderful. But the voice taunted her still.

Perhaps she had been foolish to allow herself to be used by Jacob and his father. They obviously were more concerned with saving face—and paving the way for Jacob's royal wife—than with her happiness. She wasn't sure how these things worked. Maybe no countess, duchess or princess worth her salt these days would agree to marry a prince who had fathered an illegitimate child.

But if clearing his way to the future was his only interest, why was Jacob holding her now? Why was he kissing her so tenderly, running his fingers up and down the sensitive curve of her spine, murmuring sweet words in her ear, which made her heart soar? That wasn't a necessary part of the charade. No one would know whether or not the prince and his wife were intimate.

Undoubtedly, she thought sadly, he's just taking advantage of the situation. Sleeping with women has become nothing more than a pleasant diversion for him.

Allison pulled away violently, lurched to her feet and staggered a few steps away from the bed, into the middle of the room. Glaring at Jacob, she tried to catch her breath by pulling in lungfuls of air.

"What's wrong?" he asked, looking dazed.

"Everything!" she gasped. "You...me...us! And this place that makes me feel as if I can't move for fear of shattering something priceless."

Jacob followed her glance around the room. "There's nothing here that can't easily be replaced by a copy from some designer's warehouse."

He just didn't understand. She spun to face him, her hands on her hips, ready to demand that they return to Nanticoke immediately. But she found him smiling at her, his dark eyes uncharacteristically bright, teasing.

"What?" she shouted.

"You're still intimidated by all of this, aren't you?"

"Yes, I am. So what?"

He seemed to think for a moment, although his lips remained turned up in a smile.

"I have my work cut out for me," he murmured at last, standing up. He took a step toward her.

Allison backed away from him, responding to a warning flutter down low in her stomach. She was worried by the mysterious humor in his eyes. It was as if he'd delivered the punch line of a joke, only she just didn't get it.

She narrowed her eyes at him suspiciously. "What are you talking about—your work cut out for you?"

"Come here," he said, crooking a finger at her, moving toward her again as she backed away.

"I'm not sleeping with you."

"We'll see about that. In the meantime, I don't intend

to force you to do anything you don't want to do. I just
want to talk to you."

"About what?" To her surprise, she found he'd maneuvered her around the room and was now backing her toward
the bed again.

"About *things*," he said.

"Things?"

"Yes. The princess needs educating."

She shook her head, feeling panic rise inside her, and
took one more retreating step...and the edge of the mattress
hit the soft bend behind her knees. She swallowed, staring
hopelessly at Jacob...with nowhere to run. They were married. If she tore screaming into the hall, she'd feel ridiculous and look far worse.

"Sit," he said.

She sat. Drawing her knees together inside her pink knit
dress, she folded her hands demurely in her lap and gazed
up at him, trying to look cooperative—at least until she
could think of a better plan.

"Good," he said. "You look very princess proper."

"It's a temporary condition," she reminded him.

He tipped his head to one side and looked at her as he
sat down beside her, but he didn't comment. He took her
hand and lightly placed it on his thigh, covering it with his
own. For what seemed a very long time, he said nothing.

After several minutes, he began to speak to her in the
rich, casual voice of a storyteller. "I used to think that
every female I met came equipped with a little electronic
chip in her brain that controlled her money meter."

Allison squinted up at him. "Huh?"

"From the time I was a young boy until I was off to
boarding school and somewhat on my own, I met only girls
and women who were accustomed to buying their clothing
from pricey designers and traveling the world over at whim,
all on a man's credit card. Their fathers were landed gentry,
independently wealthy politicians and powerful industrial-
ists. Many had titles that could be traced back for centuries.
These females put a price tag on everything. A couch from

a department store would never do—even if it was a practical design and perfectly comfortable. It had to be the best money could buy—imported, preferably, at great cost. Clothing, jewelry, restaurants…everything was the same. Money was something to boast about, then spend lavishly.''

"What a disgusting waste," Allison grumbled.

Jacob held up one finger to indicate he wasn't finished. "Remember, it was all I knew. The female sex was nice to the males in their lives—their fathers, uncles, boyfriends and husbands—who bought them beautiful things. The female sex was just as disinterested in and even cruelly disdainful of men who couldn't supply the goods. I believed it was the way of the world."

Allison stared at Jacob, at last understanding that he was serious. He was sharing with her something very private from his heart and life, something vitally important to him.

"So," she said slowly, feeling herself relax a notch, "when you left Elbia to go to school in England and the United States—"

"I took what I'd learned with me," he said, nodding. His left arm stretched behind her, while his right still rested warmly over her fingers, curled in her lap. "I let it be known to any girl I was interested in that I was from a royal family…and that we had lots and lots of money."

"You scoundrel," she said, then giggled impulsively at the way he wiggled his eyebrows Groucho Marx style.

"I was," he admitted. "I was incorrigible. I used my name and wealth without shame. Later, I learned to be a little more subtle to get what I wanted. And after a while, I didn't have to advertise myself at all. The press did that for me. Glitzy magazines ran Most Eligible Bachelor articles, and I was always at the top of the list. I could walk into any club, casino, opera house or embassy in America, Europe or Asia, and hear the whispers, feel heads turning to watch me cross the room. Women admired me openly and let me know they were interested."

Allison sighed. She didn't like thinking of Jacob with other women, even if he was treating his past comically.

"What does this have to do with me?" she asked impatiently.

"What I'm trying to say is, my training had paid off with every woman I'd ever met and wanted—until you. You wouldn't allow yourself to be bought. I suppose I sensed that when we were together two years ago, when Cray was conceived. I didn't try to use who I was to get you, and you wanted me anyway. You made me feel special, important…and I'd given you nothing."

"You gave me your love…at least, that's what I believed," she said softly.

"Yes, I'm sure you did believe I loved you." He looked steadily at her, as if he too was aware of how close they sat, the lengths of their thighs touching. "You'd never have slept with me if you hadn't."

She had to look away from him, blink and clear her fogging vision. The impulse to let herself weep and wash away all the hurt was nearly overwhelming. She ached inside. "I was naive," she managed in a hoarse voice, after a moment.

"Maybe." Jacob shifted himself on the bed and eased her body around and closer, so that she was leaning back against his chest. His fingers splayed over hers against the rigid muscle in his leg. "That's not my point. When I came back and told you who I was, you didn't change. You wanted nothing more from me than you'd wanted before. You practically threw a five-thousand-dollar gown in my face."

She sucked in her breath. "It cost that much!"

"Uh-huh." She could feel the muscles in his neck lengthen and knew he was grinning again, even though she couldn't see his face. "Would it have made any difference if you'd known?"

"No…yes…well, maybe," she stammered, then added defensively. "I might have donated it to the hospital for their annual auction to benefit the children's wing."

"And that's just my point," he said. "You are Allison Collins of Nanticoke, Connecticut. You aren't a woman cut out of a society mold, who estimates a person's value by the cost of the car he drives or the money he spends on her. You make me feel as if I am worth something on my own, without a title or my family's money. You liked me, plain and simple."

"Yes," she said. "I did like you, plain and simple. Just you. Just Jay...or Jacob without the von Whatever-it-is."

"Austerand. You'd better remember it—it's your name now, too."

"Temporarily," she whispered.

He seemed not to have heard her, and kept on talking. "Things...objects...they're only important or worth caring about when they teach us about people."

Now he'd lost her. "What?"

Jacob turned her back to face him. His eyes darkened urgently. "This is important. Listen. You, Allison Collins, look at anything that is worth a lot of money, and you thumb your nose at it. I agree—no scrap of cloth is really worth five thousand dollars. I wouldn't be heartbroken if the *Queen Elise* sank tomorrow, or if I never rode in a limousine again. They're just part of my life because they come with the territory—"

"Of being a prince?"

"Yes. But some of the ostentation is necessary because it keeps alive the myth—the beautiful royal family and all their glittering treasures. You see, that's what the press gets excited about, and what people like your sister get a kick out of reading about. That's what brings tourists to Elbia, and tourism is our only real industry."

Allison thought for a moment. Was he just weaving an elaborate tale to silence her objections? Somehow, it was beginning to make sense to her. "So," she said slowly, "everything your family owns or buys is just for show."

"No, not everything. It's more complex than that. You'll see when we reach *der Palast Krystall*."

"I don't speak German, but that sounds suspiciously like the Crystal Palace."

"Exactly." He grinned at her, and she was reminded of

how potent his smile could be. Her insides curled and warmed pleasantly.

"The Crystal Palace," she repeated. "Is it an amusement park or museum of some kind?"

"It is my home, and will be yours for as long as we're married."

She stared at him, the words finally sinking in. "A palace...as in castle? That's where we'll be living?"

He nodded, observing her panic-stricken expression with amused interest.

"No way," she said quickly. "Cray and I in a...a... Absolutely not."

"I'm afraid so. The palace is where the von Austerands reside when we're in Elbia. That's where you and your son will be best protected from the press and prying eyes, at least until things calm down a bit. Then we'll all have more freedom to travel and go where we please."

The panic that seized her wasn't unlike the sensation she'd felt one night at the library, when the power shut down. She'd tried to find the stairs and lost her footing. It was as if everything solid and dependable in the world had suddenly disappeared.

"Jacob, I—I can't take my baby to live in some enormous stone mausoleum full of precious art objects," she objected weakly. "At the very least, I'd be terrified Cray might break something."

Jacob still looked entertained by her reaction.

She reached futilely for a better excuse. "Tourism or not, I'll bet it costs hundreds of thousands of dollars to maintain a castle. Surely the money could be better spent on—"

His fingers pressed over her lips, silencing her protests. "The money to maintain the palace comes from the tours. Most of the castle is open to the public on weekends. The furnishings and paintings, even the architecture of the palace itself, they are our national treasures. You wouldn't have me give away my people's heritage, would you?"

Allison would never have guessed Jacob felt so strongly about anything. His family and country meant everything to him, despite the way he'd sometimes carried on, earning himself a questionable reputation. She studied the ardent lines around his mouth and the quiet pride in his eyes.

"No," she said, feeling more moved than she dared admit. "Of course not." She reached out and touched his cheek, shadowed with afternoon beard. "It sounds as if you grew up in a museum."

"It's a lot like that," he said. "I consider the palace and its treasures on loan to my family. While you are there with me, I hope you will consider them your responsibility, too."

She frowned. "My responsibility?"

"Yes. I'm offering you a job, Alli. But if you hate the idea, tell me and we'll forget about it."

She nodded, but was still puzzled by the direction their discussion was taking.

"Not since before World War II has an inventory been completed of the family's manuscript and book collections. I've tried to talk my father into hiring a professional firm to come in and do the job right, but he's been preoccupied with other matters."

Now she could guess where he was headed, and her heart began to pound with anticipation. "Yes?"

"I know how stubborn you are about taking gifts, so I figured you wouldn't be very gracious about accepting the princess's allowance. But if you're willing to take on the cataloging job, I'll see that you're paid the professional rate for your time. Of course, I realize Cray will need your attention, too, especially while he adjusts to new surroundings. So it needn't be a full-time job. And you can interview nannies and choose whomever you like to help with him."

Allison stared at Jacob in disbelief. She'd been set on hating everything involved in the next year. She'd been ready to renounce any hope of happiness until this insane part of her life was over. But Jacob was offering her a dream job, a safe and beautiful shelter, and he was trying in his own way to respect her feelings.

"This must be very difficult for you," she said, "thinking of someone else's welfare."

He looked at her as if trying to decide whether she was insulting or complimenting him. At last he picked up her hand in his and gave her a sad smile. "I guess I've never had to think of anyone but myself. It's a hard habit to break. Do you like the idea of the position as royal librarian?"

"I love it," she said sincerely. "The time will pass so much faster if I have something to keep me busy. But I have to admit, I'll be a little nervous about handling such valuable books."

He hugged her, and she could feel his heart beat through her own body. "Don't be afraid of *things,* Alli. Cherish them, as you would your own family's most precious mementos. Can you do that for me?" he asked.

"I can try," she said.

"Good." He gave her another soft squeeze.

The most amazing sensation swept over her. It was as if she was no longer a victim of circumstances. She was no longer simply along for the ride. She had a job to do.

She allowed him to continue holding her. Turning her face into the muscled swell of his chest, she inhaled his masculine scent—a mixture of aftershave, soap and flesh. His arms fully enclosed her—strong, protective. She felt an overwhelming desire to be kissed. She peeked up at him.

His eyes narrowed slightly, as if he were reading her thoughts. "Don't tease, Alli. I don't want to do anything that will hurt you again, or make you hate me more than you already do."

"I don't hate you," she said softly, as she lifted her hand and placed it lightly behind his neck. "And I have a feeling, this won't hurt at all."

He bent forward and kissed her.

She responded happily, kissing him back. His mouth hardened, pressed, then started to draw away despite the need she felt through his lips.

"No...don't stop...please, do that again," she invited him breathlessly. "After all, this is our honeymoon."

"Don't say that," Jacob warned, his voice throaty with desire. "I can't stay in this room with you and not make love to you...if you keep letting me touch you like this."

He'd filled her head with blue smoke, her body with fire. She wanted him desperately. But his words slowly brought her back to reality and the truth of who they were...and who they must remain.

Allison's eyes flashed open. She sat up on the bed and stared at him. Tension and lust swirled in his eyes. She wasn't sure how he'd held back as long as he had. Another few seconds, and they'd have crossed a final dangerous line.

Making love would only create more problems. She was a temporary princess, a stand-in who would have to step down and let the real princess take over some day. As sweet as Jacob had been about their early romance, he must think her hopeless when it came to the ways of society. He'd even found it necessary to coach her on the intricacies of being a modern royal.

"Sorry," Allison blurted out. "We kiss good, what can I say? I got carried away." Rolling away from him, she pushed herself up off of the bed. She dashed for the salon, ending up in front of the immense expanse of glass overlooking the city.

She heard Jacob follow her, but couldn't risk turning to look directly at him. When she shifted her eyes along the glass, she could see his reflection. He was standing only two feet behind her. Tall, stiff, every muscle in his body triggered—as if he were prepared to mount an assault on the enemy.

His eyes locked with hers in the glass. "You want me," he growled. "And I want you, Allison."

She shook her head sadly. "This isn't part of our agreement. I can't...won't..." There were no words to explain how much she needed him...and feared what he could do to her heart if she gave in ever again. What was the use of trying to make him understand, if he didn't know her by now? "I haven't eaten since this morning," she said dully.

"Do you think we could find some food around this place?"

Something that had been holding him together seemed to give way. Jacob's stance wobbled almost imperceptibly. His eyes dropped away from hers; they lost the hot sparks that had made them look so alive and hungry for her.

He choked out a dry laugh. "New York City had a few decent restaurants, last I knew." Before she had a chance to decide whether the hurt she'd glimpsed in his expression was real or simply a manifestation of bruised male ego, Jacob spun away, heading for the door.

Seven

"**I** feel as if I'm a fugitive from the law!" Allison scrunched down in the back seat of the taxi as it veered into the steady flow of Manhattan's evening traffic.

Two photographers ran alongside the car, their cameras flashing through the side windows. Beside her, Jacob cursed softly, but he sat erect, his chin high, dark eyes fixed dead ahead.

After a few hundred feet, the taxi sped up, leaving the press behind. Allison straightened up in the seat beside Jacob and tried to breathe in the cold, crisp winter air slowly, to calm her jumpy nerves. Lavish Christmas decorations and displays filled every store window they drove past, enticing holiday shoppers. Allison concentrated on the brilliant red-green-and-gold splashes of color, and told herself she'd get used to being rushed by reporters and learn to handle the attention with a little more grace. Maybe.

"I'm sorry," Jacob muttered irritably. "I thought a regular cab would attract less attention than a limo. I'm surprised the media caught up with us so soon. Someone must have tipped them off.'' He looked across the seat at her and took her hand in his. ''Are you all right?''

Somehow, his being upset made it easier for her. ''I'll be fine, don't worry. It was just a half dozen or so reporters. They weren't too pushy until we made a run for the car.''

He observed her, as if he was impressed by her casual tone, even if he wasn't totally convinced she was as calm as she sounded. ''I have a feeling, you'll do fine,'' he murmured. Lifting her hand he pressed his lips to her fingertips, then turned to look out the window.

Allison frowned. Perhaps her imagination was playing tricks on her, but Jacob sounded as if he was talking about something more than her ability to deal with aggressive journalists.

''Actually,'' she said, ''once I get over the intimidation factor, this might be fun. Until today, I've never been asked how it feels to be one of the richest women in the world.''

He glanced at her sideways.

She laughed and let her fingers nestle deeper within his. She wasn't even sure he was aware they were still holding hands. A habit, she supposed, that he'd picked up with his other girlfriends. ''Don't worry,'' she said, ''I won't get greedy. When it's time for me to step aside, I'll do it. And you don't have to pay me a fortune.''

''We'll see about that,'' he said shortly. And once again, she wondered if she wasn't reading more than one meaning behind his words. He was a far more complex man than she'd once thought.

The traffic moved more slowly as the taxi turned onto Broadway, heading south. Cars jammed every intersection. The driver shot a look up at the rearview mirror. ''Thought you looked familiar, mister. You that royal fella they been yakkin' about on the radio?''

''Radio?'' Jacob's voice seemed suddenly pinched.

''Yeah.'' The man pushed his cap back on his balding head and turned the volume knob on the dashboard. An announcer was talking about a meeting at the United Nations, then he gave the Dow-Jones report. ''They'll come to it again,'' the driver muttered. He broke off to loft a few colorful expletives at another cabby who awkwardly cut him off. "Keep repeatin' the same stuff all day.''

The announcer finished reading the stock market report. "Well, ladies,'' he crowed, "weep a tear…weep a tear! One of the richest bachelors in the world is out of the wife market. In fact, he's apparently been a married man for almost three years. Sources at the *New York Times* revealed just hours ago that Crown Prince Jacob von Austerand of Elbia, the second smallest country in Europe, secretly married his college girlfriend that long ago. And they have a son. For reasons known only to the royal family, the marriage was kept secret until now. The prince and princess are right here in the Big Apple, celebrating a second honeymoon, and will soon fly to Elbia where they and their son will live at a level of luxury most of us only dream about. Sorry, gals!''

Allison stared at Jacob. He looked white as a sheet.

Then, for some reason, she felt like laughing…and she did. Loudly. "Well, I suppose that makes things a lot simpler. Someone let the cat out of the bag for us.''

Jacob ground his teeth. "Resnicek's people. Someone at his office must have run to the *Times* with the story. If I find out who—''

Allison laid her hand on his arm. "It's not necessarily bad. We were going to announce our marriage at the press conference anyway. They could have leaked the truth, then we'd have a real problem.''

"I suppose,'' he admitted.

The cab pulled up in front of a tall limestone building. It looked like just another office tower, but a discreet canopied entrance was labeled with a small brass plaque that read: La Fleur.

Jacob looked up and down the street. "At least no one's waiting for us here. Come on, let's get inside before someone spots us.''

Allison scooted across the seat and out the door. Jacob paid the driver and tipped him generously, then joined her on the sidewalk. She glanced past him at the cabby's alert expression. He was grinning as he screeched off down the busy city street. She giggled.

"What?" Jacob asked, taking her arm and leading her down a flight of steps to a dim grotto of a lobby, glittering with sconces made to look like dripping candles.

"I have a feeling we'd better eat fast," she said.

"Why?"

"Bet you any money our chummy driver is heading for the nearest pay phone, where he'll call a buddy reporter and sell out our location."

Jacob stared at her incredulously. "You certainly catch on fast."

She laughed. "This *is* sort of fun—like playing Bonnie and Clyde without all the shooting."

He shook his head in amazement. "I'm glad you're enjoying yourself. Maybe you can keep me sane through all of this."

The maître d' did a marvelous job of keeping prying photojournalists out of the dining room. But every once in a while, from outside in the reception area, there came a sudden flurry of scuffling sounds and raised voices. And Allison knew another member of the press had been ejected by the pair of neckless bouncers installed near the front desk when they'd arrived.

Jacob and Allison ordered and ate each course without seeming to rush, but she barely tasted her rich dish of sea scallops, shrimp and lobster tail swimming in a luscious lemon-butter-wine sauce. The fun of eluding the press faded as old worries returned.

"What are you thinking now?" Jacob asked. He reached across the table and touched the tips of her fingers with his. Now that the word was out, she supposed he expected her to play the loving wife, for the public eye. All tender touches and puppy eyes.

She sighed, trying to pretend she felt nothing from his warm fingers. "Cray," she murmured.

"He's with Diane. He'll be fine."

"It's not that. She's a whiz with kids. I'm concerned that the gossip about us is going to spread."

"Of course it will. Like wildfire. I told you to expect that, for a short time."

"What if some reporter tracks down Diane's address before we can get back to Nanticoke?" she asked.

Jacob scowled at his plate, took a forkful of medium-rare filet and chewed thoughtfully. "That might be a problem. Do you want to telephone and warn her?"

"I think it would be better if we just got home as soon as possible," she suggested. "Do we still need to do the press conference scheduled for tomorrow?"

"Not a formal one, anyway. It will be better if we answer a few questions and let them take pictures, to get their editors off their backs. Then they won't be lurking around every corner, waiting to jump us. I'll put in a call to Frederik, just to let him know there's been a change in plans." He thought for a moment. "It won't do us any good to drive back in your little car, since our cover's been blown. Are you very attached to it?"

"My little rattletrap? Not really. It gets me around. Most of the time."

"Would you mind if we gave it a new home? Donated it to a worthy cause?"

"Right now? Here?"

"If I call Thomas now, he can drive into the city and have the limo at the hotel by the time we finish with an impromptu meeting with the press."

"Sounds like a plan," she said.

Jacob was impressed. Although he'd always sensed a natural strength and courage beneath Alli's seemingly meek exterior, he had nevertheless expected an adjustment to public life would take weeks, maybe even months. He was charmed by her attitude.

Later that evening when the press corps gathered in one of the hotel's chandeliered ballrooms, Alli handled herself with remarkable ease. Even the most jaded reporter in the room smiled back at her when she turned her sparkling aquamarine eyes his way. After thirty minutes of whirring videocams, blinding electric strobes and shockingly personal questions, Allison still looked relaxed and radiant.

"I didn't get a chance to say so earlier," Jacob said when they were finally driving out of the city with Thomas at the wheel of the limousine, "but you were amazing back there."

She laughed. "I was hardly amazing. I was so nervous I thought that pompous society columnist in the front row would hear my knees knocking together."

"Well, even I didn't hear them." He brought her fingertips to his lips and kissed them delicately. "You make a breathtaking princess."

Her eyes dulled and the smile left her lips. "Don't say that."

"Why not?"

Allison's glance snapped up defiantly to meet his. "You wanted me to marry you for a purpose, to clear the way for your future. I'm still just a small-town librarian who's playing a role in a little melodrama you and your advisers have cooked up."

"You're far more than that."

She looked up at him wide-eyed, as if terrified of the warmth he'd tried to put in his voice for her sake. He had to remind himself that he couldn't tell her everything—not now, not until he'd worked out every complex detail. He didn't even know if what he had in mind was possible.

In a way, he realized he was being selfish again—but this time he felt no guilt. He was determined to get what he wanted, and he was willing to risk everything—his father's approval, his countrymen's love, Allison's treasured independence...perhaps even more.

Allison tried to draw her hand out of his. Her reluctance to let him touch her reignited the lust that had gripped him in the hotel earlier that day. His fingers locked around hers.

"You know the way, don't you, Thomas?" Jacob called forward.

"Yes, Sir."

"Carry on, then." Jacob reached out with his free hand and pushed a button to close the privacy partition between his chauffeur and the expansive passenger area.

"Jacob," Allison said, warning in her voice. "Don't."

"Relax, I'm not going to seduce you. Unless," he added wistfully, "you'd enjoy—"

"No," she said firmly. "I'm going along with this fantasy of yours for purely practical reasons. I'm *not* your mistress. I thought I made that perfectly clear before."

"There's one part of this that isn't fantasy," he pointed out, observing her smugly.

"Oh?"

"You are my wife. Everything's perfectly legal." He leaned back into the richly padded leather seat, contoured to curve across the back and around one side of the vehicle's interior, and grinned at her. "Wouldn't you care to take advantage of your matrimonial rights?"

"I married you to foil the press. I didn't say I'd sleep with you because of them, too."

"Consider our making love as a means…to foil our mutual lusts?" he asked hopefully.

Allison glared at him. "In a limo?"

"Ah, she didn't say no…she countered with a question. I sense the woman is weakening." Jacob loved sparring with her like this. She was an adorable challenge, a worthy adversary. "If not here, then how about in your cozy four-poster bed when we get home?"

She cast him a look of pure disdain. "Forget it, Your Royal Highness."

He sighed, and decided to change tactics. "I won't press you. I wouldn't want you to do anything you found distasteful." He leaned away from her to give her the illusion of space, but his arm stretched out lazily over the back of her seat. "Sorry, if I stepped out of bounds." He plucked a strand of pale hair from her shoulder and twirled it between his thumb and middle finger. It felt like silk. He wanted to seize handfuls of it and thrust his face into the honey-colored strands.

She ignored the intimate gesture, cleared her throat and spoke with the rigidity of a dedicated nun addressing her class. "I understand. I suppose for a man like you who has been freely intimate with half the female population of the world—''

He laughed. "Now that's a bit overstated! A lot of what gets into gossip columns is just that—gossip.''

She tilted her head prettily to one side and observed him as the car sped down a ramp onto the interstate. It had started to rain, and the tires hissed on the wet pavement. "But you've been with a lot of women. And you said they don't often turn you down.''

"True,'' he mused, "but it's not as if I go to bed with every woman who smiles at me.'' He played more aggressively with her hair, gently brushing her scalp with his fingertips, then moving them down to her nape. She stretched out her neck, like a cat relishing a good scratching from her master. "Feel good?''

"Mmm...''

"How about this?'' He massaged the top of her shoulder.

She rolled her shoulder muscles, pressing up against his hand. "That feels marvelous. All the tension just...just evaporates. Other one?''

Jacob turned sideways on the seat to face her, and she rotated her hips so that he could get both hands on her back. He continued talking to her about everything inconsequential and nonthreatening that came to mind. His own running patter began to make less and less sense to him, but it seemed to form a soothing accompaniment to the motions of his hands as they moved over her shoulder blades, down the sweet hollow of her spine to the narrow span of her waist just before her hips swelled enticingly, invitingly, irresistibly...

The hum of the highway beneath the limo was a distant reminder that they were speeding along at seventy miles an hour, but Jacob wondered if Allison was at all aware of where she was. He peered around her shoulder and her eyes were closed.

"I feel like…like…" she murmured, as if from the depths of a trance, as her head dropped limply forward.

Holding his breath and praying he wouldn't break the spell, Jacob bent forward and touched his lips to the sexy curve between her shoulder and nape. "Like what?" he whispered.

"Like I've left my body and I'm floating somewhere…up there." She tipped her head an inch toward the window and the darkening winter sky. A few snowflakes drifted down around the limo, mixing with the rain, clinging to the warm tinted glass for a second before melting.

"Is it nice up there?" he whispered.

"Yes," she said. "Oh, yes."

He risked another feather-light kiss on the perfect patch of skin just above the neckline of her dress. Her flesh quivered beneath his lips. Instead of lifting his lips away, he kept them pressed against her flesh and inhaled her flowery scent.

He told himself this was as far as he'd intended to go. All he'd wanted was to touch her, feel close to her again…maybe get a little rise out of her, pleasurably shock her. He had every intention of honoring her wish to not sleep with him…for the time being. But something inside of him that was basic and male and as undeniable as truth, demanded both her softness and her sex. She'd given him all of herself, before. He couldn't forget or stop wanting to return to that place they'd shared.

While his lips skimmed over the alabaster-smooth skin at the base of her neck and his hands worked magic up and down her sides, he shifted his position subtly once more. He held his breath as his hands came around her ribs to smooth warmly upward, over her stomach. With the lightest pressure, he coaxed her backward until she rested against his chest.

Jacob didn't dare touch her breasts. Not yet. Her eyes were closed and her breathing slowed, as if she was drifting off to sleep. He kept his hands moving slowly, comfortingly over her, in the same way he'd learned to settle his hunting pups when they'd been frightened by a thunderstorm. Stroking. Petting. Gentling her.

"Nice," she murmured on a long, whispery breath.

"Um-hm." He experimentally outlined the dip of her navel through her dress with one fingertip.

She didn't object.

He let his hand slide lower, as if it were merely carried by gravity, as if he had nothing at all to do with its movement. He let his palm settle over her skirt and shape itself over the angle between her thighs. He didn't move his hand. He held his breath and waited again. But her body didn't tighten, her hands didn't push him away...and she said nothing.

Jacob sensed that if he spoke again—whatever spell he'd succeeded in weaving would be shattered. But he wanted a signal from her, some sign that she was open to receiving the pleasure he so wanted to give her.

At last, he could wait no longer. His fingers slowly gathered up the pink wool folds of her skirt, working their way toward the hem until he found a different texture. Panty hose. Still she said nothing, did nothing to stop him. But he felt a slow tremble beginning to build from deep within her body. It was so subtle at first he could see no external sign of it as she leaned, seemingly relaxed, against him. But he knew how she'd be, if she let him continue. He remembered the pattern of her passion, how her female hunger intensified when they made love. And it filled him with wonder that she'd kept all of that desire inside herself, releasing it only for him. No other man had made love to her.

Knowing he must act now or not at all, Jacob moved his right hand upward and beneath the elastic of Allison's hose, then down again, until he'd inched his fingers beneath her panties. He found lace, a thin strip of satin, then the soft curls between her legs that he remembered being nearly as blond as the long strands brushing his cheek. He stopped himself from moaning with his own pleasure. This was for her, just her. He could wait if he had to.

The tip of his first finger gently moved between the first moist folds, until he touched the sensitive bead of flesh he sought. For a moment, he didn't let his hand move at all. Then he pressed gently...then a little more firmly, before beginning to flick his finger back and forth, until he felt her react to every brush stroke of his fingernail across the pliant button. He teased it, tormented it. She squirmed interestingly in his arms, her lips pursed in concentration, her eyes squeezed more tightly shut. She moved her legs apart another centimeter and moaned his name.

It was all the invitation he needed.

Slowly...slowly, he told himself.

Jacob stroked her with exquisite sensitivity, reading the least sigh from her lips, the smallest twinge from her body, repeating any motion of his hand that created pleasure for her. He wanted to make her pleasure last as long as possible. But he found that isolating himself from the act to let her have all the fun, wasn't possible. When her body tightened and writhed on a wave of ecstasy, he felt a strong answering surge through his own body, that settled like fire in his loins.

Still he controlled himself, concentrating on lifting her slowly through layer after layer of fiery bliss. He couldn't take his eyes off of her face. He watched in fascination as her expressions changed with kaleidoscopic variety and beauty from supreme exultation to blissful relaxation, then again to a fierce need for him to not stop what he was doing to her. She gripped his arm with both hands and her nails dug into the muscle, but he didn't flinch.

He pushed his finger deeper, circling and probing and stroking her, until he knew the least motion would send her over the final edge.

He ached to taste her when she erupted, but knew she'd never allow it. Not here...now...in this car as they sped across the dark landscape—even though they were fully screened from the world.

Very quickly, he lifted and turned her to straddle his lap, then pressed two more fingers into her, hard. She tightened around him, arched her back, opened her mouth and eyes wide. Before she could cry out in euphoria, he pulled her head down with his free hand and pressed his mouth up to cover hers, stifling the whimpers that accompanied each flow of heat and moisture he felt within her.

But Jacob didn't let her rest for long. He understood the needs she'd kept locked up inside her for so long, needs that were still waiting to be released. He brought her to a soaring, fiery climax two more times before he was certain he'd satisfied her. Then he held his breath, fearing her silence, for she hadn't said a word the entire time he'd made love to her with his hands.

Allison moved only enough on his lap to settle her dress back into place, then she rested her head on his chest and her hand on his thigh and sighed very deeply, as if she had just polished off a double hot fudge sundae with whipped cream, nuts, cherry…the works. "Jacob?" she whispered.

He held her close and hoped for the best. "Yes?"

"Did *you?*"

"No." He smiled. Not that he couldn't, even now, in a flash. Still he felt strangely satisfied, as if he'd shared in her release.

"You realize, you've broken your promise."

He stopped smiling. "I'm sorry. I didn't mean to—"

"You've spoiled everything."

"I only wanted to—"

She touched her fingertips to his lips. "Hush. No excuses. What's done is done. You'll just have to pay the penalty." She paused and he felt his world dissolving around him in a sad blue mist. "Next time," she continued, faintly, "I shall seduce you."

He grinned broadly. "Anything you say, darling."

Eight

Allison had believed that Christmastime could never be more beautiful than in Connecticut. She had grown up in a world of silver birch and evergreens dusted with snow, frosty drifts slicing across fields of corn stubble, icicles glistening in a wintry sun as they dripped from red barn roofs, and the mouthwateringly sweet smells of deep-dish apple pie, cinnamon snickerdoodle cookies, maple-pecan fudge and roasting turkey with herb stuffing. But Elbia in early December simply took her breath away.

"It's a dream world," she whispered, gazing out the window of the von Austerand family's helicopter at the fairy-tale scene below.

They'd flown the Concorde as far as Paris. Jacob had arranged for the helicopter to meet them at Orly for the second leg of the journey. Elbia had only one airport, with runways too short to accommodate jet craft. The family used the racy-looking high-speed chopper for quick, comfortable transport to major airports or for weekend shopping trips to cities such as Vienna, Berlin or Rome.

"The Crystal Palace," she breathed the words. "It's obvious why it's called that."

Jacob leaned across her to point out the window at the slender stone turrets below. "They look like icicles, don't they? In the sunlight."

"Yes," she said. "And the walls sparkle. Is everything covered with ice this time of year?"

"No, that's mostly an illusion. The marble was quarried in Russia, during the fifteenth century, from a narrow vein of rare white stone streaked with quartz. It catches the light, like crystal, and reflects it. When the land around its base is covered with snow, the effect is magnified. You'd swear the whole structure was made of glass."

"What a beautiful illusion," Allison murmured, leaning back in her seat. Her relaxed posture was just as deceptive as the stone. She felt on pins and needles—eager to leap from her seat as soon as they landed, to investigate every tower, wing and gallery of the castle below. But another part of her warned her to scurry for safe and familiar ground, if any could be found in this strange land.

This is not your world, an internal, cautionary voice reminded her, again and again—these are not your kind of people; they will destroy you. How could she carve out a year or more of her life and live in such splendor, then submissively return to her old life and be satisfied? It would be impossible. But even if she had refused to accompany Jacob back to Elbia, the world knew about Cray and his father. Things would never be the same. It was all out of her hands.

She looked down at Cray, strapped into the seat between her and Jacob. He was playing with Jacob's wallet. When they'd boarded the helicopter and it had risen sharply into the air, his eyes had grown wide with terror and he'd clutched at Allison. Nothing she did comforted or calmed him. Jacob had hastily looked around the inside of the plane, but found nothing to distract the little boy. With an inspired grin, he pulled out his wallet and held it up to Cray.

For some reason, the object intrigued the little boy as much as the doeskin gloves on the day they'd met. Cray reached out greedily for the new toy, stopped crying and became absorbed in studying its pockets, flaps and the plastic cards and pretty-colored paper money inside.

"You're going to have a tough time reclaiming your property," Allison said, nodding at her son.

Jacob smiled. "He's the only person in the world I'd let have it without a fight. Amazing, isn't it?"

"What?" she asked.

"He has no concept of money or the value of things. All he really cares about is that you, his mother, are here with him."

Cray slapped the leather billfold against Jacob's knee then peered up at him impishly, as if to observe his reaction to the personal contact.

"I think he's getting used to having you around," Allison remarked.

They'd delayed their trip so that she could find a real-estate agent to handle renting her house while she was gone. Although the usual red tape would have made it impossible for her to get a passport in less than six weeks, the Elbian embassy had pulled magic strings, and with the cooperation of the U.S. State Department produced the necessary papers in a few days. Alli had also talked Jacob into giving her more time so that she could sort through the house with more care—pack the things she most needed, put furnishings and family mementos she'd want later in storage. During those two weeks, both Jacob and Thomas had stayed with her in the beach house. Thomas had spent most of his days chasing off reporters and celebrity voyeurs. He looked exhausted now, as he dozed in a forward seat beside the pilot.

"Pretty soon," Allison mused, "he'll add your name to his vocabulary."

"I wasn't aware he had a vocabulary." Jacob's eyes seemed to melt as he observed his son.

"Oh, he does," she said firmly. "I can understand him, clear as a bell."

"Do you hear that, Thomas?" Jacob said, leaning forward to poke his friend in the arm. "Little Cray will be saying my name soon."

Thomas cast his boss a dry look, over his left shoulder. "And what will that be, Your Royal Highness?" he said.

Jacob's expression dimmed. "I hadn't thought." He looked at Allison.

"Jacob," she said firmly. "That's your name."

"Why not...Dad?"

She didn't like the stubborn glint in his dark eyes. "No."

"Why not? I *am* his father, after all."

"I could strangle you for bringing this up now, Thomas," she grumbled.

The bodyguard shrugged.

"It's something we should have decided before now," Jacob continued, laying his wide hand on Cray's chubby leg. There was a touching tenderness in the gesture that Allison wished she hadn't seen.

She sighed and said quickly, "I didn't think it would come up. After all, a few years from now Cray won't even remember you." She concentrated on the dramatic view of snowcapped mountains ringing the castle. Beneath its soaring walls, red tile rooftops flanked winding, narrow streets lined with shops and stone cottages that looked centuries old. If her heart hadn't been hammering out a desperate warning in her chest, she would have savored the view.

"Daddy," Jacob whispered playfully in Cray's ear. "Can you say D-a-d-d-y?"

Allison could have cheerfully killed him.

The helicopter circled the crenellated stone walls. Within them was a formal garden, brown and dead this time of year. At the far end of the maze of paths, there appeared to be a landing pad that had been cleared of snow. The plane set down with a reluctant wobble, like a big bird that felt more at home in the sky than on land. Jacob unsnapped Cray's seat belt.

Before Allison could object, he grabbed Cray, wallet and all, ducked through the door in the curved belly of the helicopter and under the blades, then dashed down a path toward an archway in the castle proper.

Thomas helped Allison retrieve Cray's diaper bag and step down to the ground. In the second that they stood alone in the roar of the blades, he turned to her. "Stand by him!" Thomas shouted. "He needs you!"

She stared up at the big man, trying to figure out if she'd heard him right. But the urgency she thought she'd heard in his voice and seen in the fleeting tension of features mostly obscured by heavy beard was gone.

"Come along, Princess," the Englishman said in a more normal volume as the helicopter's engines cut to a dying whine. His eyes shifted meaningfully but unemotionally toward the castle. "His Royal Highness is waiting for us."

She balked, seized his sleeve to stop him. "There's something more happening here than what I've been told. Isn't there?"

"Now's not the time," he rumbled. He bent nearly double and hustled her out from beneath the still-spinning blades.

"Later, then," she said hastily. "I know you're absolutely loyal to the prince, Thomas. I've seen the way you two are when you're together. If you love him as I do, please tell me what's going on."

"Just stand by him. Be brave. Don't give up too soon." He looked across the garden toward Jacob, who was holding open a massive wooden door beckoning for them to hurry. "I can say no more. Let's go, Princess—it's freezing cold, you'll catch pneumonia."

Allison obeyed him, but she tucked away his strangely troubling words, knowing they'd return to her later. She decided she'd find a way to steal some time alone with Thomas and confront him again. If Jacob had secrets, he would keep them to himself unless he chose, for his own reasons, to give them up. She'd learned he was a bull-headed man, even more so than many. He was not easily swayed once his mind was made up, nor would he be made to share his feelings. But Thomas seemed to like her, and she sensed there might be ways of convincing him she needed to be told the lay of the land for her own protection.

The entire staff was waiting to greet their new princess in the dim wood-paneled salon where Jacob led her. They were courteous and smiled so enthusiastically they might have been waiting years to meet her. She realized with a sense of shock that this was, in a way, true; there had been no lady of the house since Jacob's mother died.

Allison greeted each man and woman—from downstairs maid, to master cook, to third assistant butler. As she moved along the line of uniformed servants she was aware of Jacob, still holding Cray, watching her with increasing interest. She wondered if she was passing or failing a test he'd set for her.

"When will I meet your father?" Allison asked when she reached the end of the line and Jacob had dismissed the staff, leaving just the four of them alone in the room. Her, himself, their child…and Thomas.

Jacob and his friend exchanged quick looks. "It will be a while," Jacob said shortly.

"Won't he be having dinner with us tonight?" she asked.

"I expect not." A subtle note of irritation sounded in Jacob's voice. "He's been very busy," he added quickly. "Come along. I'll show you your room, then you'll want to see the library and the—"

Allison planted her feet and folded her arms over her chest. "Jacob," she said bluntly, "there's something wrong here."

Cray must have sensed tension in the air. He started to whine and stretched out his chubby arms toward her. She took him from Jacob and cuddled him to her shoulder.

"Nothing's wrong," he insisted. "I just know my father. It will take a while for him to accept what's happened."

"He's angry with you for marrying me?"

"Furious is more like it. But it's not the marriage as

much as—'' He let the words drop away unspoken, but his eyes told her everything. They shifted expressively from her to Cray.

''I see,'' she said. ''You weren't careful enough in your games. You created an embarrassment to the king, is that it?''

Jacob didn't answer. Instead, he turned to Thomas. ''You can go. Take the rest of the day off, you need the rest.''

Allison waited only until the other man shut the salon's iron-studded wooden door behind him. ''So, what does your father intend to do? Hide himself from me and his grandson forever?''

''My father doesn't hide from anyone, believe me,'' Jacob said tightly. ''He's just biding his time and letting us both know how displeased he is. When he's ready he'll appear. I don't look forward to that moment,'' he admitted.

Allison stared at him. ''Are you actually *afraid* of your father?''

When Jacob's eyes met hers, they were blazing with black fire. ''Never! I've never been afraid of him or walked away from a battle with him. That's probably why we haven't gotten along all these years. I won't crumble, which is what he wants.''

''Then why this charade? I thought he forced you to marry me.''

''No. The wedding was Thomas's suggestion and my decision.''

''But why did you do it?'' she cried, more confused now than minutes before. ''Is this out of spite for your father? To make him angry? If so, I think that's being very childish.''

Jacob glared at her in exasperation. ''I told you before, Alli, I've brought you here as my bride, to protect you. As to any more personal motives...I don't feel obligated to justify myself to you or anyone else. Producing a marriage certificate to wave under the nose of the press might have been Thomas's brainstorm, and it did appeal to wily old

Frederik, my father's adviser. But that doesn't mean I'm blindly following orders or acting out of childish whim."

Allison had never seen Jacob this angry. His entire body seemed consumed with the effort to not grab her and shake her. She sensed she'd only make things worse if she pushed for more from him.

"I'm not sure I believe you," she said quietly, patting Cray's back and rocking him against her breast as he sucked his thumb for comfort. "But I suppose now that it's done and we're here, all I can do is wait things out."

He nodded stiffly, swung around and headed for the door. Allison looked around. It suddenly struck her that if she didn't stick with Jacob, she was sure to get herself lost in the immense castle in no time. Clutching Cray tightly she scrambled after Jacob, into a foyer hung with fringed banners, coats of arms and marble busts that looked ancient. She looked up, saw him ascending a gracefully spiraling stairway and took off after him.

They arrived on the second floor in a long hallway lined from floor to ceiling with mirrors. The visually spectacular effect of reflections in endless repetition made the corridor looked miles long. If it had not been for the thick wine-colored carpeting covering the stone floors, the passageway would have felt cold and unfriendly. But the rich hue created a deceptive warmth, making the overwhelming amount of space seem almost cozy.

"This is our room," Jacob said, opening the first door on the right.

Allison hesitated in the doorway. "Our?" she repeated, hiking Cray's diaper bag higher on her shoulder.

Jacob looked at her as if she were extremely short on brain matter. "Yes. It's expected that the prince's wife share his bed."

She rolled her eyes. "Jacob, we agreed that we wouldn't be lovers. That thing in the limousine...it was exciting but...well, don't think of it as part of a pattern for us."

"What about your statement about you seducing me?" He fixed her with an ebony gaze she couldn't avoid.

Allison felt her cheeks blaze. "I'm sorry. I let myself get carried away by the moment. I shouldn't have." The fact was, in the time since their drive back from New York, she'd kept herself and Jacob so busy that there had been little opportunity for them to make love again. And then Thomas was with them in the house, and it was a very little house.

"It just…just can't happen again," she sputtered. Why couldn't she find the right words to make a convincing argument? Remembering how Jacob's hands had felt, bringing her soul to life as he had, muddled her thoughts. Even her breathing altered, becoming quick and shallow. "I assumed in a place as big as this, there would be plenty of room for me to have my own bedroom."

He took her arm and moved her inside the room, then shut the door behind them. "It won't work," he said.

"Why not? I really think—" She drew a sharp breath as she took in her surroundings. "Oh, my…Jacob. Oh!"

The room was vast and spectacular. Actually, the word *room* failed to describe the sweep of space before her. She stood in a private suite with sleeping, dressing and bathing areas. At the far end, in a windowed semicircle that might have been part of a turret, was an adjoining nook for lounging about or entertaining that was complete with a love seat, two comfortable-looking upholstered chairs in pale blue-and-white striped chintz. A graceful, low Queen Anne table stood between them and on it sat a pedestaled silver bowl, overflowing with fresh fruit. The bed, a distance away, was of a dark, heavy wood that might have been mahogany or cherry. It was piled high with a down-filled comforter and tons of fluffy pillows encased in cream-colored satin to match the ecru crocheted coverlet. Beside the bed were delicate crystal lamps and shelves of leather-bound books, titles embossed in gold leaf. The volumes looked temptingly old, incredibly valuable. Her fingers itched to pick them up and examine them.

"This is magnificent." She sighed.

Cray started wriggling in her arms and whimpering softly.

"I'm glad you like it," Jacob said, relieving her of the diaper bag. "This used to be the royal bed chamber, my parents' room. But after my mother died my father preferred to take a smaller suite in the east wing, closer to his office."

"I feel as if I've died and gone to heaven," she said, trying to quiet Cray. His movements became frantic.

"Put him down if he wants to play," Jacob said, indicating the thick expanse of pastel flowered carpet. It looked like an Aubusson, although she'd never seen a real one as large.

"He's exhausted...all of this traveling," she murmured. "He really should have a nap."

"The nursery's right through here." Jacob led her toward a double-wide door that looked new. It was louvered, to allow sound and air to pass through even when closed. She wondered if he'd personally ordered it installed. He must have understood she'd want to be able to hear Cray if he cried in the night. "Do you want to lay him down? He might as well get used to his new surroundings."

She walked through the open doors into another room, so sweet it brought tears to her eyes. Everything was blue and white, from the crib to the curtains and carpet. Shelves of toys and books ranged up one wall. Soaring windows let in dazzling sunlight along another. A climbing gym rose in the center of the room.

"You must have had people working in here round the clock," she said.

"Do you like it?"

"Yes. Yes, I do." But already her practical nature was kicking in. "I'm afraid, though, he'll never sleep with all this light."

Jacob reached toward a panel of switches and flicked one. Opaque shades lowered themselves with a soft mechanical hum, all along the window wall. He touched another pad and a night-light snapped on, before the room was blanketed in soothing darkness.

Allison shook her head in amazement. "This will do, I guess." She took a bottle she'd kept as a traveling spare from Cray's diaper bag and held it up to him. "Thirsty, big boy?"

He grinned lopsidedly at it, his eyes already looking heavy in the dark room.

Jacob left the bag with her, then stepped outside while she settled Cray down for his nap.

Allison fed and changed Cray, calmly going through the usual routine. But inside, she felt torn by a dozen different emotions. She felt sincere thankfulness for Jacob's thoughtful preparations for her and her son's stay with his family. He'd provided a wonderful place for them to live, rooms where Cray would be safe and could grow, learn and enjoy himself. Rooms she could relax in and retreat to for privacy. It seemed Jacob had thought of everything, from her taste in decor to the beautiful antique books at her bedside.

But Allison was disturbed by the intimacy of the arrangements. She would share this delightful room with Jacob. He didn't actually believe she was going to let him sleep in the same bed with her every night, did he?

As tired as she was from their travels, she knew she couldn't put off talking about her concerns. Her mouth suddenly felt dry, her palms moist, when she left the nursery and reentered her suite. Jacob was sitting on the love seat, one long leg crooked over his other knee, a book propped between them. He seemed to be concentrating on his reading, unaware she'd reentered the room.

"Jacob," she said softly, moving around to the back of the love seat. She touched him lightly on the shoulder when he didn't respond. "Jacob, we need to talk."

"I believe this is a first edition," he commented. "You might want to check it out when you get around to cataloging the books in the main collection. I bet the decorator just pulled these out of the library, thinking they looked

old and artsy. But this one, at least, could be of consider-
able value.''

Allison sighed. "Jacob, put the book down." She rested
both hands on his wide shoulders and stared down at the
top of his head. The dark hair was raven-wing black. Like
the smoothly arranged feathers of a great bird, the short
strands glistened and settled perfectly into clipped layers
down to the neatly trimmed nape. She longed to run her
fingertips through his hair. A pleasurable shiver raced upward through her core and she had to shut her eyes for a
moment to steady herself. The warmth of standing so close
to Jacob brought back intimate moments. Times like this,
she too easily imagined their hands promising wonderful
things to each other's bodies.

Jacob set the book on the chair arm and tilted his head
to look up at her. "What is it? Something you need that I
forgot?''

"Yes," she said. "I need you to get out of here."

He scowled, and his body tightened defensively. Only
then did she realize how cold she must have sounded.

"I didn't mean it that way," she said quickly. "I just
don't think…Jacob, you can't possibly intend to sleep in
the same room with me."

"I don't see why not," he replied easily. "There's plenty
of space in that king-size bed. We might have to do something about adding another closet, but I can get a carpenter
in tomorrow if—"

"Jacob, stop it!" she hissed, aware of Cray sleeping in
the other room, trying to keep her voice low, although she
felt like shouting out her frustration at the top of her lungs.
"You know exactly what I mean."

Reaching up, he took her hand and pulled her around the
love seat to the front. "I know precisely what you mean,
and you're not getting away with it." With a quick tug, he
brought her down onto his lap.

"Getting away with what?"

"You're not isolating yourself and our son from me."

A dangerous tingle worked its way along her limbs.

"You said I had to come here to avoid the press and keep Cray out of the public eye, for his own good, for my entire family's sake. I understood that. But living in the same building, especially one as large as most hotels, is completely different from sharing the same bedroom with you!"

"Sure is." A smile teased his lips, and she realized he was enjoying himself. His arms closed snugly around her waist.

"Jacob!" she fumed. "I thought the arrangement was clear. We're doing this for practical reasons. I can't be married to you and start acting like...like a married woman—"

"You mean by making love every night when we go to bed?" he supplied innocently.

"Yes! That's exactly what I mean...I can't do *that*, then months from now casually hand you off to some other woman."

"Why not?"

The question took her totally by surprise. Diane was always accusing *her* of being naive. Was he even more unaware of the power of the heart than she had been?

"Why can't you just have sex with me, then let me go?" He was taunting her and she could see that now. She wasn't about to let him win at this game.

"Because it's not morally acceptable to me," she stated flatly.

"Oh," he said. His hands moved up over her sweater as if smoothing out the wrinkles. "Then it has nothing to do with your being in love with me—because that's the most obvious reason a woman wouldn't be able to let a man take another woman as his wife."

"In love with you?" She gasped. "After what you've done to me?"

"Yes," he said, his voice low, "in love with me."

The passion-etched scratchiness in his voice brought back heady, wonderful moments. She felt weak, slightly dizzy, subtly achy...totally vulnerable.

"When we made Cray," he whispered, "we trusted one

another. We made love without reservation or thought for the future.''

"But that was then!" she cried. "Before you...oh, Jacob, you know there's nothing to negotiate. You can't stay married to me and take over the throne from your father.''

"That would seem to be true," he agreed.

"And you're not willing to give up your right to lead your country, are you?"

"That's also true," he replied solemnly.

"So there can be no future for us."

He didn't reply, but the muscles across his face tightened. "Now isn't the time to talk politics."

"This isn't politics," she said furiously. "This is what's happening to *us*. Now. It's very personal." She struggled to get up, but he wouldn't let her slide off his lap.

"Stay put, dammit!" he snapped.

Allison froze, fearing the sudden harshness in his voice and the rock-hard tension in his arms, which bound her. She stared at him, wishing she could see past the shade of secrecy he pulled down over his eyes whenever he didn't want her to read his thoughts.

At last he spoke, grinding out the words between his teeth. "I'm sharing these chambers with you, as you've said, for practical reasons. How long do you think this pretense of marriage would last, if word got out that the prince and princess had immediately taken separate bedrooms?"

She laughed nervously. "In a place as huge as this? Jacob, for goodness' sake—this is literally a fortress! How would a reporter get past your security system, guards and all these servants?"

"A reporter doesn't have to get *in*," he pointed out. "We employ 165 in our staff, including secretaries, groundskeepers, maids, butlers, cooks and security staff. People gossip. They go home to their spouses and friends and discuss the goings-ons of the royal household...and you'd better believe that even the most discreet among them sometimes slip up and talk to the wrong person. We have to make this marriage look real in every possible way."

She closed her eyes briefly as her body shuddered at his meaning. "You can sleep on the love seat."

"Too short. I'll get a backache from contorting my body to fit it."

"*I'll* sleep on the love seat."

"I wouldn't have it," he countered. "Can't you trust me?"

She didn't answer, but realized with an embarrassed jolt that her fingertip was drawing figure eights across his shirt-front. She could feel the rise and fall of his breathing, could trace the bands of muscle and tight hollows between them. She pulled back her hand and inhaled sharply.

"I see." His eyes widened and he grinned. "It's not a question of your trusting me to leave you alone. You don't trust yourself!"

She playfully slapped his chest. "You wish."

"That's it, isn't it?" he teased. "You can't bear the thought of lying in the same bed with me and not being able to make love."

"Stop it, Jacob!" she cried. "You're not being funny, at all."

"Oh, no? Well, let's just try out this bed and see what happens."

"No!" she shouted, as he stood up abruptly and she slid off his lap. He hauled her up into his arms before she could hit the floor and strode quickly to the bed. "Jacob, no...please...I can't do this...."

"Do you mean you can't lie on a bed with me without tearing off all your clothes and begging me to make love to you? Why not? Because you don't love me? If that's so, just say it. Say the words, Allison. I'll leave you alone. I swear I won't touch you if you just swear that you have no feelings for me."

He bent and flung the covers off the bed, then dropped her onto the mattress. Allison tried to sit up, but a mass of feathery pillows swallowed her up. "It's more complicated than that!" she cried.

"No, it's not," he said firmly. "Some things in life are

complicated, others aren't. Love isn't, not really. You either love a person or you don't.''

He lowered himself onto the bed beside her and pulled her close. His breath caressed her face. His body molded itself to fit hers. She could feel his heart beating against her breasts. His firm, hard stomach pressed against hers. And lower down…he was aroused. Very aroused. She felt the air around her thicken and swirl, confusing her thoughts, making reaction…any reaction impossible.

How could she admit to him how deeply she cared, when he took their relationship so lightly? When he found it so easy to walk away from her whenever it suited him?

His hand moved between them and found her breast through her sweater and bra. His palm smoothed over her. Pressed. Fighting off the steamy sensations that battled against her sanity, she turned her head to bury her face in the hollow of his shoulder. Jacob lifted her sweater and slid his hand beneath it, then under her bra. He cupped her bare breast. He suckled her raised nipple.

Allison arched and quivered at the blaze of sensations his touch summoned from her.

"Tell me you don't love me and I'll stop," he whispered in her ear. His moist breath clung to its rim. His words shimmered with a promise of ecstasy she could too easily recall.

I don't want you to stop! her mind shouted.

But thankfully, her lips wouldn't move. She hated herself for being so weak. Love him? Of course, she loved him! She'd loved him from the first day they'd met in Nanticoke and she had never stopped. Even during the times they'd been apart, even as she'd cursed him for leaving her…she'd known that she loved him. She was destined to hold in her heart forever this one, maddening, exquisite man—despite fate having pitted itself against them.

But just as surely as she loved him…he *didn't* love her. He loved his country. He loved his title and the power it gave him to buy or do whatever he wished. And it was that power that would allow him to use her now.

"I don't love you!" she shouted out on a sob.

His hand stopped moving, his breathing quieted. It was as if all the life had rushed out of his body.

"I see," he whispered, the two tiny syllables seeming to take immeasurable effort. "I guess I expected too much."

"I'm sorry," she uttered dully, although she couldn't have said why she was apologizing. You asked for a person's pardon when you'd hurt their feelings. How could she have hurt Jacob if he didn't love her?

Slowly, he pushed himself off of the bed and stood with his back to her. He settled his shoulders, straightened his spine and smoothed his tan sweater and slacks.

"Jacob, I—"

"You don't owe me an explanation," he pronounced coldly. "You said the words. I asked for them. That's enough."

"But it's not that—"

"I will trouble you as little as possible, but there's nothing to be done about sharing the room. Don't worry about being attacked during your sleep. It won't happen."

He never turned back to face her before walking out of the room. She didn't see him again until after midnight when he let himself soundlessly into the room while she pretended to sleep. He undressed, but for his underclothes, and took for himself a slender edge of the bed on the far side from her. He never once touched her, even in sleep, all night long.

When she awoke in the morning from a shallow, agitated sleep, he was already gone.

Nine

Much of the next three days Allison spent unpacking, accustoming Cray to his new home and investigating the confusing maze of hallways that connected over one hundred rooms in the palace. Finding the family's everyday dining room—there were two other larger formal dining rooms for special occasions—became easier. She memorized the route between her suite and the library and soon felt confident enough to investigate other areas of the building.

One afternoon she took a wrong turn and strolled through a door that opened into the central courtyard with its desolate winter-browned gardens. The door latched behind her before she could slip back inside. Allison wrapped her arms around Cray to shield him from the icy wind. She pounded on the door and called out, hoping someone would hear her before the baby caught cold.

Almost immediately a young voice called to her in German from beyond the doorway. "I'm coming! Patience...patience, now!" When the door swung open, a teenage girl stood in the opening. Her irritated expression turned to dismay. "Your Royal Highness, oh, dear, come inside before you and the babe freeze!"

"I'm sorry to trouble you," Allison murmured, frustrated with herself. "I'm afraid I took a wrong turn, and before I realized my mistake I was locked out." She brushed a flake of snow from Cray's pink nose. "The gardens look huge. I'm looking forward to walking through them in warmer weather."

"Ah," the girl said. "In the summer, the flowers are so beautiful. The king has a fondness for roses. His gardeners tend the bushes all spring and summer and into the fall. Never have you seen such a beautiful sight. You like gardens?"

"I love gardens," Allison said, smiling.

The girl, who wore a maid's uniform, grinned back at her, then turned to observe Cray, who was batting his long, dark lashes at her and drooling prolifically for her benefit—the ultimate compliment.

"What's your name?" Allison asked.

"Gretchen," the girl said. "He is a beautiful, handsome baby. He looks like his father. So strong. And he has kind eyes." She giggled. "Kind and wicked sometimes, too." She blushed, apparently shocked that she'd been so bold in front of her mistress.

"It's all right." Allison laughed and shook her head. In centuries past, a servant might have been whipped for such personal comments. "You're right. Kind but wicked. My Cray is always up to mischief, I'm afraid." She hesitated only a moment. "Would you like to help me take care of him? I need a nanny for him, if I'm to be free to get any work done around here."

"Work!" The girl looked puzzled. "But a woman who marries a prince, doesn't—"

"This one does, because she wants to," Allison interrupted her. "Maybe American women are different. At least I am... I have to keep busy. So what do you say?"

The girl gazed adoringly at Cray. "Oh, yes," she whispered.

Allison scheduled two hours later in the day when she could talk at more length with the maid. She'd immediately liked the girl. Cray seemed to have taken to her, too.

Having concluded her preliminary interviews for a nanny, there seemed to be no getting around talking to Jacob. She couldn't simply pluck the girl from her other duties without clearing it with whomever arranged the staffing. And she had no idea who to talk to about that.

Then there was the matter of the girl's pay. Besides, Allison felt oddly compelled to discuss her decision with Jacob on other grounds. As the baby's father, she felt he should have a say in who would care for his son. And he knew the staff far better than she. He'd be able to tell her if Gretchen was as bright and reliable as she seemed.

But talking with Jacob would be so very hard. She felt his hostility whenever they passed in a hall and while they sat across the table from one another over a meal. He avoided her most of the day, but when they ran into each other he put on a show of civility toward her, for the benefit of any staff who happened to be within hearing. The leaden color of his eyes when he looked at her chilled her to the bone. She couldn't honestly believe that she'd hurt him by telling him that she didn't love him. Yet there seemed to be no other explanation for his behavior. Unless it was purely a matter of male pride. Men like Jacob, she supposed, weren't used to being turned down.

She found him in his study, a room lined with bookshelves, which seemed a smaller version of the richly paneled library where she had started working a few hours a day while Cray played on the floor. Her job was to record each of the thousands of books by title and author, then estimate its current value. The process was a slow one, especially since she had to entertain her energetic son while working. But with Gretchen's help she hoped things would go faster.

"Excuse me, I don't want to interrupt your work," she said softly, after knocking and hearing his quiet summons from inside. "I need to consult with you about Cray's nanny."

"No problem." Jacob sat up stiffly and closed what looked like a ledger on the desk in front of him. "Have you interviewed women from the town already?"

"I don't think that will be necessary." She told him about Gretchen and added that she'd left Cray with her in the nursery for a short while, so that they could talk.

Jacob toyed thoughtfully with a gold pen. He made a point of not looking directly at her. "I know the girl," he said at last. "She seems a hard worker and dependable. Gretchen has been coming to the castle to help out with her mother since she was twelve. You couldn't have picked a young woman with a better temperament. She's never anything but cheerful. But I don't know if she's had any child-care or teaching experience."

"I'm more concerned with her attitude than her professional qualifications," Allison explained. "When he's not with me, I want someone with him who is loving and protective. Someone who enjoys playing with him. He'll be able to sense he's more than a job to her."

Jacob nodded, still focusing on desktop, pen, his hands, the window...everywhere but on her. "Fine. But I want it understood that I will be spending time with him too—every day," he added firmly.

Allison frowned, surprised. "Of course, if you like."

"He's my son," Jacob said. "I want to be part of his life."

There was something universally human and touching behind his detached tone. Allison felt braver than she had for a long time. She stepped forward and laid her hand over Jacob's on the desk blotter. "Of course, you can see him...any time you like."

He jerked his hand out from beneath hers, as if she'd poured scalding water over it. As he glowered up at her, hate filled his nearly black eyes.

She swallowed and found her voice. "Jacob, you asked

me to say what I said. You pressed me until I had no choice.''

"Don't patronize me!" he lashed out, rising from his desk so abruptly he knocked the heavy high-backed chair against the wall with a thud. "The girl will do fine. I'll let our chief of staff know of the change, so that she can be replaced for household duty."

Allison stepped forward. "Jacob...I wish—"

"Get out!" he bellowed. "I have work to do. You've got what you wanted, now leave me!"

Allison couldn't walk away from him in the state he was in. The pain she read in his eyes was real. If it was only pride she'd crushed by denying her love for him, it was the kind of pride a man needed to survive. As deeply as he'd hurt her, she felt responsible for hurting him.

If there was one thing she'd learned since she'd been in Elbia, it was that a lot of people depended upon Jacob. Although his father was king and ruler, on paper, of the little country, a lot of the day-to-day work had already been turned over to Jacob. He spent twelve or more hours each day in meetings in the east wing, which she'd learned was where all the government decisions were made. And when he was done there, he closeted himself in his personal study to read, study reports and proposals, and prepare for the next round of meetings with his father's cabinet or foreign dignitaries. He worked hard for his country, but all the world knew of him was the wealthy playboy.

Her heart melted to see him suffering so deeply, and all—it seemed—due to her.

"I don't understand," she whispered. "Jacob, tell me why you're acting this way."

"There's nothing to tell," he stormed. "I have work to do, woman. Get out and let me do it."

"No," she said stubbornly. "Not until we really talk."

She refused to be cowed by his vicious tone or by fiery glares meant to intimidate her. As quickly as she chased after Cray when he made a crazed dash for a flight of stairs, she rounded Jacob's desk and stopped in front of him—daring him to push her aside.

She could see the heat rising in his face as he stared down in disbelief at her. She could feel the tension in his body, stretching his muscles so taut they might snap at any moment. The veins in the backs of his hands stood out as he repeatedly clenched his fists at his sides.

"Get out of my way," he growled. "If you won't leave this room, *I* sure as hell am going to."

"Not until we talk," she insisted, forcing her voice to remain strong. "I don't want you to make love to me because—"

"Because you hate me. I understand that—I screwed up your life. I knocked you up, then dumped you."

"No!" she shouted at him. "Shut up and listen to me... Your Royal Highness."

He looked vaguely surprised and less sure of his ground.

Impulsively, she took his big hand in hers and held it tightly. His fingers flinched and he attempted to tug them away, but she refused to let go. "I can't let you make love to me again because I don't think my heart could bear to lose you one more time. And I know that's inevitable. It will happen because too much is stacked against us."

Jacob observed her with interest but not trust.

She dared to step closer to him, bringing their hands down between them. "Jacob. I did love you once... I think I'll always love you, although I hate myself for allowing you to have that much power over me." Tears quickly filled her eyes, spilling down her cheeks. "When we met I thought you were just like me—an ordinary person. I imagined you finishing your degree, getting a job—hopefully near Nanticoke. We'd be married and live there, start a family. Just like my parents—two ordinary people who loved each other."

"Well, you were wrong," he snapped.

"Yes, I was. Totally wrong. I can't ask you to give up everything you have and are. And as long as that's the way it is, we can't plan a future together."

"You're right," he said tightly. But by then his eyes had softened. "Do you mean what you just said?"

"About not being able to plan a—"

"No, about having loved me...always loving me."

She nodded. "But it's no good if it's a one-way road...if you don't love me."

"Whether I might love you or not is immaterial," he stated, coldly.

Her face felt as if it were suddenly afire with shame. Tears trickled down her cheeks, no matter how hard she fought to stop them.

He pulled himself up so that he seemed to gain six inches of height. His eyes were hard and determined, the pain disappearing into hidden recesses. "I *will* take the throne," he said firmly. "And I *will* have you. I have no intention of giving up either."

Allison knew she couldn't possibly have heard him correctly. "I told you, I won't be your mistress. That's no life for me—sharing you with another woman, living apart from you and spending my days wondering when I'll see you again...if I'll see you. It's no life for Cray either, having a sometimes father."

His arms moved quickly around her trembling shoulders, and he pulled her close to him. "Alli, what's done is done. We have a child. We've been lovers and created a life from our bodies. Whether you like it or not—you have feelings for me. And I have feelings for you—we won't go into what they might be now." His words came out in a rush, as if he were afraid something would stop him from getting them out. His arms tightened around her possessively and held her. "I'm not the kind of man who settles for less than everything. I will find a way to keep you and keep my title and keep Cray."

He was talking nonsense...wild impossibilities... miracles. Jacob was like a little boy who'd never been told *no*. He didn't understand that the world operated under its own set of rules, which were beyond his power to change. She'd never feel complete, existing as "the other woman'' in a shady corner of his life. What of the family she'd hoped to raise? She didn't want Cray to be an only child. What of her poor parents, who were already so upset by all that had happened? And how would Jacob's father and the people of Elbia feel, knowing he blatantly kept two families? It was all so impossible.

She opened her mouth to protest.

He hastily covered her lips with his and kissed her to silence. "You're mine," he said, allowing no argument. "You made a mistake just now when you admitted you love me. I was ready to let you go, thinking you didn't care. But now I won't give you up, Alli—not for anyone or anything."

The iron inflexibility shining in his eyes was frightening. "But I can't—"

"You don't have to do anything," he said. "The rest is up to me. It may take a while, but..." He let the thoughts troubling him go unspoken. "In the meantime, I'm going to have fun being a father. And I'm going to very enthusiastically enjoy being your husband."

She bit down on her lower lip to stop it from trembling. He had given her not one inch of ground to stand on. He hadn't told her he loved her. In fact, he had evaded defining what he meant by the feelings he claimed for her. Then he had sworn he would give up neither his title, nor his right to a royal wife, nor his son. She wondered if, after signing the marriage contract in New York, she had any legal rights at all. Perhaps she should have read it more carefully.

But before she could give her position before the law any more thought, Jacob bent over her and pressed his lips possessively to hers. He kissed her long and deeply.

Allison found herself incapable of resisting. She melted in his arms. She was emotionally drained, to the point of feeling powerless to fend him off. If he wanted to take her here and now, on his desk, on the floor—she wouldn't fight him. In a way, it would be a relief after the past tension-filled weeks.

Jacob's warm, moist lips possessed hers again. He

moved his tongue over the ridge of her lower teeth and
tasted her hungrily. She responded, opening her mouth a
little wider, letting him know that she wanted him too and
would open the rest of herself to him.

There was a knock on the door. Without waiting for permission, a thin charcoal-suited figure stepped into the study.

"Frederik!" Jacob's voice was sharp, ringing with his
displeasure.

Allison quickly tried to step out of Jacob's arms, but he
held her fast.

The old man's eyes settled only briefly on her, then
drifted away as if she were of no more interest than a piece
of furniture. "You have a meeting with the minister of
finance in five minutes, Your Royal Highness," the man
announced.

"Yes. Yes, I remember."

Allison could sense Jacob trying to control his anger over
the ill-timed interruption. At the same time he must have
been fighting to rein in his raging libido. He still had his
arms around her, as if unwilling to release her.

"I'd better go and check on Cray," she murmured, looking up at him, trying to communicate her discomfort with
the situation.

"I suppose so," he said slowly. But his eyes locked onto
hers meaningfully, as she stepped away from him. "I'll see
you later. Wait up for me."

As soon as she stepped out of the room, leaving Jacob
alone with his adviser, she leaned against the wall in the
hallway and counted very slowly to ten. Then she started
counting all over again. After a minute or two, her
breathing calmed, and her pulse no longer pounded dangerously. There was no doubt in her mind what would happen that night.

Reassured by her admission that she loved him, Jacob
would claim her as he intended to claim all that was his
birthright. There was little she could do about it. The force
of his will would sweep everything before him, including
her. Strangely, the thought excited her, but she was equally

aware of how perilous loving a man like Jacob could be.
She only hoped they'd survive their passion and that she'd
have a shred of her own life left when the flames finally
died.

Jacob held himself together through the afternoon meetings. He couldn't have said how he did it. The minister of
finance was a tough, savvy negotiator with a long list of
budget reforms. She'd always reminded Jacob of Maggie
Thatcher, whom he'd personally known, loved and feared
since his boyhood schooldays in England. Serious problems
had to be discussed. Decisions that affected his people had
to be made. By sunset he, the minister and their staffs had
agreed on what they could, had worked out a few compro-
mises and initiated a study to look into further refinements.

But every minute of every hour while they'd argued and
fought over what was best for Elbia, he'd thought of Allison. The emotions he'd seen on her sweet face flashed per-
sistently before him. Her steely determination to have her
say when she'd first entered his study, colored by specters
of fear when he'd raised his voice to her. Her intensely
loving gaze as she'd confided her true feelings. Her barely
concealed sexuality as she clung to him, looking implor-
ingly up at him, begging him to understand why she
wouldn't be satisfied with being just his mistress.

He hadn't been able to sleep for the three nights since
Alli had told him she didn't love him. His ego had taken
a nosedive, of course, but there was more to it than that.
He'd felt like a brute for forcing himself on her, for trying
to talk her into giving up her personal convictions and resume sleeping with him. Once he'd been able to give her
pure and intense pleasure, without their future haunting
every moment they were together. But he sensed that every
time they made love from this day forward she'd be holding
a part of herself back, fearing what was to come. He hated
himself for doing that to her. But for now he had no choice.
He only prayed that each crucial step of his plan would fall
into its proper place when the time came.

But time was getting short.

As soon as Jacob was alone in the conference room, he looked at the clock. It was after 5:00 p.m., but Alli might still be working in the library.

He strode into the water closet and splashed cold water on his face, then ran a comb quickly through his hair. Moving fast, he headed down one hallway, then another, automatically taking the right turns to take him into the private oldest section of the castle, where the family library and living quarters were located. The library door was closed, which meant someone was probably inside.

Jacob pushed anxiously through the door. "Alli? You here?"

Thomas looked up from the table where he sat, documents and aging books spread within arm's length. He removed horn-rimmed eyeglasses, looked up from the book he was reading and pinched the dented pink spot on the bridge of his nose. "She left almost an hour ago."

Jacob scanned the room. Stacks of books had been pulled down from the shelves and arranged in an unfathomable order. "Looks like she's been busy."

"Yes," Thomas said. "Very, I'd say."

Jacob started out of the room, then had a second thought and turned back. "What are you reading there?"

"Just an old novel Allison...I mean, Her Royal Highness recommended. I thought, a little quiet time before dinner, if you don't need me?"

"No, of course, please go ahead," Jacob said, waving his hand in release. He was pleased the two of them were getting along. Thomas didn't usually make an effort to get close to the other women who had breezed through his boss's life. "I, um—may not see you at table tonight." Unlike most of the other servants, who ate together in the kitchen, Thomas was considered a companion to the prince as much as an employee. He had a standing invitation to all family meals.

"Working late again tonight?"

"Something like that...yes," Jacob mumbled, closing the library door behind him.

He felt as if he were being driven by an internal engine, one that had kicked into overdrive and refused to settle into a complacent idle. He needed to find Alli, to be with her. He needed to touch her and reclaim her as his alone, forever. And now that he finally understood her feelings better, he knew what he had to do to accomplish that.

Jacob rushed down one corridor, turned a corner, ran down a second long hallway lined with oil portraits of his ancestors painted by masters whose other works could only be viewed in the Louvre or the British Museum. Rembrandt, Bronzino, Dürer and Ingres, at one time or another had painted von Austerands. In another minute he was breathlessly dashing up the stairs, two and three at a time.

Without knocking, he burst into the bedchamber he shared with Allison. His heart raced with anticipation of seeing her. He stepped into the middle of the room and in one rapid glance took in the bed, reading corner, dressing table and lavish bath with its sunken pink marble soaking tub and soft gray-and-pink fixtures and tile. She wasn't anywhere within the suite. His heart fell with a sickening sensation.

Then he heard a gentle, nearly inaudible sound coming from the nursery. Was it singing?

Unable to restrain himself Jacob broke into a run, but stopped short at the doorway. The sight before him took his breath away—Alli in a pure white cotton dressing gown, lace-collared, flowing in loose ruches to her ankles. She was rocking Cray in the chair beside his crib, softly humming a lullaby.

Her long blond hair swept down over her shoulders and disappeared behind her shoulders, where it was tucked between her back and the chair. Her head rested against the wooden spindles and her eyes were gently closed. He told himself he should wait patiently outside the room until she put Cray down, but he couldn't stay away from them.

Walking on tiptoe, feeling just a little foolish for doing

so, he crossed the room. It smelled of baby powder and Allison's perfume. When he stood beside them, he wasn't sure what to do, so he just stood there not saying a thing, just enjoying feeling a part of his little family.

"I don't normally put him down this early," Allison whispered, somehow knowing he was there without opening her eyes. "We played tag for two hours to get tired."

Jacob grinned at her and gently rested a hand on the little boy's head. His son snuggled contentedly, deeper in his mother's arms. "His mother looks as worn out as he does."

Her eyes flashed open, sparkling blue, alive. "I'll get my second wind soon enough."

He was overpowered by the throaty passion in her voice. He couldn't remember a woman he'd ever wanted more, had ever wanted to hold onto for more than a few nights or weeks. They'd all come and left so easily. As if blown to him, then away on a capricious zephyr. But Allison had haunted him, clung to his heart even when she'd tried to make him believe she didn't love him.

Now he knew the truth.

Now he would show her all he could not say.

She settled Cray in his crib and covered him with a light blanket, even though he was completely covered by fleecy footed pajamas. Jacob took her hand and they walked out of the nursery together, backs straight, eyes straight ahead. He quietly closed the doors to the baby's room, knowing they'd still be able to hear him if he woke during the night. Jacob felt only a little guilty for hoping Cray slept like a rock.

"Are you hungry?" he asked, still keeping his voice low.

"Not really." She looked up at him, almost shyly, as if they hadn't made love before. "Maybe later...we could have something brought up?"

"Absolutely," he said. "Anything you like."

They stood facing one another in the middle of the room. She studied his face with detached wonder, as if she were learning him all over again, starting with the visible parts—his face, his hands.

"Undress me," he whispered.

She blinked at him, looking a little surprised, then tilted her head to one side and replied impishly, "Okay."

He had fantasized about her doing this for him many nights as he lay awake during the years they'd been apart, then again, just the night before. He had delighted in the memory of her graceful, delicate fingers—loosening his tie, unbuttoning his dress shirt, tugging the hem from his pants. He'd grown excited at the imagined gritty vibrations of his zipper and her tiny hands coaxing his pants down over his hips. And he always pictured himself standing before her in just his briefs, waiting patiently, smiling devilishly at her, daring her to make the next move, watching her expression as she became aware of his erection barely contained by the taut cotton fabric.

Then he'd close his eyes and conjure up the sensation of her hand slipping inside and holding him. Usually, that was as far as the fantasy went. Without her actually being there, giving him a reason to hold back…he couldn't.

But tonight, he had a reason to control his most basic male urges. Although he could easily have reached his climax simply by looking at her, he checked himself.

Jacob watched her eyes as Alli watched her own hands working off his clothing. She shot little glances up at him, now and then, as if to be sure he was paying attention. He paid great attention. He was full and hard and eager for her before she reached the middle button of his shirt. By the time she was unzipping his fly, he was nearly frantic for her.

With his clothes at his feet, Jacob stood naked before her and let her look at him for as long as she liked. "Take me in your hand…please," he asked, ever so politely. He smiled. "It's chilly in these castles."

"Then we should warm all of you, not just this," she said as she curled her fingers around him.

He thought he was absolutely going to burst. "Not yet," he said as much for himself as for her. "I want to see all of you, too."

Jacob took his time, but he could sense she was not only willing to allow him to disrobe her, she was impatient for him to take away her gown. Impatient, too, he suspected, to discover what else he had in mind for them.

It was amazing to him that she chose to trust him one more time, after all he'd put her through. Yet she did. He could tell she wasn't simply giving in to him because he'd put her in an impossible situation. She was telling him with her eyes and the soft motions of her fingertips and the little high-pitched sounds that escaped between her lips that she wanted him to make love to her. This wasn't the predatory female lust he'd seen in other women's eyes. Allison wasn't having sex with him. She was making love. And for the first time in his life, he fully understood the difference.

It was as if she read his mind. "I want to love you in every way possible," she whispered, her breath sweet and giving against his ear.

"That's a lot for one night," he teased.

"I mean it, Jacob. I've decided it's today that matters." She took his head between two small hands and held him back from her just long enough to fix him with her startlingly sea blue eyes and make him understand that she was serious. "Today you're mine, and I'm yours. We'll make the minutes count."

"And how will you handle tomorrow?" he asked, worried because he could conceive of a fragile side of her shattering if things didn't happen the way she wished.

"I'll face tomorrow when it comes," she murmured. "If we are together, that's all that matters. Any other situation that forces itself on us... I'll survive and so will you, though perhaps not happily. But I refuse to let this kind of joy be destroyed by fretting over something that might or might not be around a corner."

As she spoke in her mesmerizingly liquid voice she stroked his whiskered jaw, traced the clipped line of black hair bordering his temple, touched his eyes adoringly. The brush of her skin against his was soothing, as calming as her words, reassuring him that there was nothing she wouldn't do to be with him.

If another woman had tried to be this open with him, he would have felt threatened. He would have known she craved his wealth or was pursuing him with the hope of using his power for her own purposes. He would have fled and never looked back. But Allison had a way of letting him know that it was *he* who mattered, not the things he could buy her. And behind her words hovered an undeniable sense of destiny he'd already felt himself—a manifest force that had lured him back to her twice.

Love? He wasn't sure that was what he'd call it, at least in his own case. He still wasn't certain he was capable of loving a woman in the way the great poems and romantic ballads described. But it was clear to him that an undeniable force was drawing them together, an energy far stronger than his family's blueprints for his future. He felt compelled to fight for his right to possess this woman, whom he wanted above all others.

Jacob clasped Allison's hands in his and held them tenderly, like two butterflies captured in a gauze net, as he eased her toward the bed. He knelt in the middle of the thick comforter and she knelt facing him.

"I'm glad," he said, simply, though there was so much more he knew he should be telling her. "I'm glad you're not shutting me out of your life, although I've given you more than enough cause. You'll never know how sorry I am for the pain I've caused you, my darling Alli."

Her eyes filled with tears. "Oh, Jacob...the hurt, it's just..." She shrugged. "How can it compare with the joy?"

On that cue he took her in his arms and laid her down on their bed. They made sweet and savagely beautiful love into the deep and magical hours of the night, relearning all the sensitive secret places that drove them to ecstasy, pleasuring each other slowly, repeatedly to make the night last an eternity. Each time he came inside her she seemed to glow more brightly. Her essence became unearthly, her body accepted his and seemed to become a part of him...just as he became one with her.

At last, both blissfully sated, they lay in each other's arms and slept the shallow dreamless slumber of lovers, holding each other as though needing reassurance that what had happened was real, forever, and nothing could take from them what they'd freely given and received. But as exhausted as he was, Jacob could not really sleep, because he knew the risks he'd soon be taking to keep Allison and his son with him. The battle would not be an easy one.

Ten

Allison woke to the pungent aroma of fresh coffee. The air in the room beyond her toasty covers felt chilly, but the fragrant brew promised warmth. She opened her eyes, somehow already knowing Jacob had left their bed and the suite. For a moment she was distressed by his absence, then she saw the note.

Propped against a silver coffee carafe on the nightstand, along with a pretty flowered Wedgwood cup and saucer, creamer and sugar bowl, was a small square of pale blue paper. Written on it in manly, square letters were words that made her heart sing—

Darling,
Hope your dreams were sweet. Breakfast is waiting in the dining room. The coffee's to fuel your lovely metabolism from here to there. Don't worry about Cray. I fed him his breakfast. More accurately, he played Van Gogh and I a piece of canvas. More of his cereal

ended up on me than in his tummy. I could get to
enjoy this fatherhood business! I asked Gretchen to
take care of him this morning until you are ready for
him. Have a beautiful day—I'll see you tonight. Hopefully, for dinner. Definitely, for time to ourselves.

Yours,
Jacob

Allison breathed in deeply and let herself fall back into
the mountain of satin-covered pillows. How thoughtful of
him to let her sleep. And how wonderful it was to hear that
father and son had spent time together. She looked at the
clock over the fireplace. It was nearly ten. She couldn't
remember sleeping as late since the days before Cray was
born. What a luxury!

Sighing, she propped herself on one elbow and poured a
cup of steaming coffee. It was a rich, aromatic brew, much
heartier than American coffee. She had liked it when she
tasted her first cup on the night they'd arrived. Now she
couldn't imagine going back to the weaker grocery-store
varieties from home.

That was sort of the way it was with Jacob, she mused.
After loving a man like him—so strong, complex, over-
powering in personality and presence—how could she ever
find another man even vaguely appealing?

Allison treated herself to a second cup before venturing
from beneath the cozy bed linens, then took a third with
her into the combined bathroom and dressing area. After a
quick shower and blow-drying her hair, she chose a cuddly
chocolate-colored angora sweater and matching leggings.
The dark shade offset her long blond hair. She was intentionally staying away from pastels these days, because the
books she was working with invariably were covered in a
layer of dark, gritty dust that seemed magnetically attracted
to clothing.

As soon as she was dressed, she went into the nursery
to check on Cray. He was sitting on the platform of his

climbing gym, with Gretchen perched cross-legged beside him.

"*Guten Morgen*," Gretchen called out cheerily. "His Royal Highness said you were very tired and I should stay with the baby so that you could sleep."

"Thank you," Allison said, grinning. "I really appreciate it."

"*Es macht nichts.* It is nothing at all, Princess," Gretchen said, giving Cray an adoring squeeze. "Little Cray, he is the handsomest baby in Elbia. And he's so smart. He already knows all about books, how to hold them carefully and turn the pages."

Allison rested her chin on the edge of the wooden platform and made a face at her son. He giggled and mimicked her. "I've read to him since he was born. He loves books."

"I will read to him in English *and* German. That way, he will learn both languages at the same time."

"That's wonderful. Please do." Allison hesitated. "I want to work in the library for a few hours before lunch. Will you stay with him until then?"

Gretchen bobbed her head enthusiastically. "Cook will send up my lunch along with Cray's. But you should go shopping, not work, Your Royal Highness. In town, there are many *Kleidergeschaften*—how you say, boutiques? Dress shops?" She looked pointedly as Allison's casual leggings and sweater.

Allison laughed. "So castle folk don't approve of American leisure wear? Well, I suppose I can make some concessions. But every so often I'll just have to lounge around in my sweats."

"Sweats?" Gretchen looked horrified, as if Allison had just told her she was contemplating smearing her body in mud and strolling through the castle.

"Yes, you haven't lived until you've spent a whole day in a sweatshirt and sweatpants." She shook her head at the girl's doubtful expression. "I'll buy you a set for your day off."

Allison left the suite smiling to herself. It was going to

be fun, after all, learning about palace life. She tripped lightly down the marble staircase to the first floor. From the foyer, she could hear voices and the shuffling of feet. Many feet. She'd forgotten it was Saturday. On weekends, she'd been told, public tours traipsed through select areas of the castle. Tourists and townspeople weren't allowed in the bedchambers, or in Jacob's and the king's private offices, but they were led through many of the other rooms which housed priceless furnishings from various periods of the castle's existence, starting as early as the fifteenth century.

She waited for the group to pass, then crossed the formal entry hall, with its elaborate wall sconces and immense gold-and-crystal chandelier high above her, to the library. The door was closed. Undoubtedly, she thought, to shut the room off from the tour. She swung it open and stepped through, still preoccupied with Jacob's romantic note and holding inside her the warmth of his promise for another night of love. Only as she was closing the door behind her did she hear two male voices and realize she wasn't alone.

She immediately recognized the gaunt figure in the charcoal business suit. "Oh—I'm sorry. I didn't know you were here, Frederik," she apologized quickly.

Jacob's elderly adviser observed her without smiling from where he stood beside an immense stone fireplace, ablaze with flames. The heat waves seemed to dance around him, polishing the dusky fabric of his suit to an orange glow, deceptively setting his face in motion with each flicker of flame.

"*Guten Tag*…miss."

She had noticed he never called her *Princess* or *Your Royal Highness* as the rest of the staff did. "Good day to you, too. I was going to work on the cataloging again this morning, but if you're in the middle of a meeting, I can come back later."

For the first time, the other figure turned to observe her. He was a large man, carrying a lot of weight, with the splotchy complexion of an individual in poor health. His hair was silver and sparse. His suit, like Frederik's, was impeccably tailored. When he observed her, his eyes narrowed with serpentine attentiveness, taking in every inch of her. He said nothing.

Frederik stepped forward. "Yes, you'd better come back."

"*Nein!*" the other man roared, emphasizing his displeasure with a cutting motion of his hand. "There will be no better time."

Allison frowned, confused for only a moment by the man's stormy mood, before she spotted the telltale crest on his gold-and-ruby ring, identical to the one Jacob wore. She was about to meet Karl von Austerand, Jacob's father...her father-in-law...Cray's grandfather. King of Elbia.

Her mouth went dry and her hands shook uncontrollably. She knotted her fingers together in front of her. But when her body urged her to step submissively backward, she forced herself to move forward.

"Your Royal Highness," she said through tremulous lips. "I'm so glad to finally meet you." She extended her hand to shake his, but he merely stared at it. She performed a quick dip of a curtsy, thinking maybe that was a more appropriate gesture.

Karl still didn't move. His mouth remained firmly pressed into an unyielding line.

Frederik cleared his throat and spoke in a thick accent. "The king has asked me to address you on his behalf. You must realize by now that Jacob's love affair with you was very foolish, a political disaster for him."

"Foolish?" she repeated, suddenly aware of the hostile direction the conversation was headed.

"Yes. He was to have assumed the throne on the first of the year, after a Christmas wedding. That cannot happen as long as he is married to a commoner."

"I understand all that," she said slowly. "He's explained your traditions to me. But what I don't see is how my marrying him makes him a poorer leader?"

The king glared at her as if she were the stupidest female on earth. His face grew redder.

Frederik said impatiently, "It is *das Gesetz*...our law. If the eldest son of the king marries a commoner, the throne goes to the child next in line. There is no other son—or daughter, for that matter. Jacob is an only child. He must rule or there will be chaos."

"It sounds like a very outdated law," she snapped, flustered at being cornered by the two men, but unwilling to let them have the satisfaction of bullying her.

"That's not for you to say," Frederik said. "The point is, Jacob is an intelligent man, although he may succumb to passion too often for his own good. He realizes he cannot sacrifice his country for a fling with a woman of no character, no family. A foreigner!"

Allison stared at the two men, trying to convince herself she wasn't hearing the words that were ripping through her soul. Could it be possible that these men, who had seen Jacob grow from a baby to the man he was today, knew him better than she?

Frederik drew himself up confidently and looked down his beak of a nose on her. "My dear, I'm sure this pains you greatly. But don't deceive yourself, Jacob will make the right decision in the end. He has agreed to an appointment with a young woman of noble parentage, from Venice, on the day of the Christmas Ball. He will ask her to be his queen and—"

A strangled cry seemed to tear itself from Allison's throat. "But he's married to *me!*"

"That's inconsequential," Frederik retorted, looking irritated at her interruption. "He will divorce you as soon as it is socially acceptable, and marry the countess. There must be a short delay, of course, before the arrangement can be made public. But the details of the new match have already been worked out. Jacob is a good boy. He will do what is necessary."

"And your *good boy* has agreed to all of this?" she

whispered hoarsely. Her head rang; her eyes burned with tears she refused to shed in front of these arrogant men.

When Frederik seemed to hesitate, the King answered in surprisingly clear English. "Of course, he has. He's known what was expected of him since he was a boy. Do you suppose he would turn his back on his heritage and countrymen because of a silly American girl who got herself into trouble?"

Anger scorched away the hurt and bitter disappointment that, moments earlier, had shattered her fragile happiness. "*I* got *myself* in trouble? It seems to me, your son had a lot to do with it!"

Karl observed her through disturbingly familiar eyes— the exact color and shape of his son's. His voice softened. "Young woman, has my son told you he loves you?"

She swallowed. "I—I *know* he does."

"Has he *told* you?" he demanded. "Has he said those words to you?"

She pressed her lips together. No, he hadn't…not once. But she couldn't admit it to these two powerful men who held her and Jacob's destinies in their hands.

"I thought not." Karl sighed. "My son and I have not always seen eye to eye. But I know Jacob. He has married you because he feels responsible for the child. That is his only reason. There have been women before you…many women. And there will be women after you, my dear. You'll be much better off realizing that now. A year is too long for you to stay here. The sooner you leave Elbia, the sooner you will be able to start your new life."

Hot tears filled her eyes. She was no longer capable of fighting them back. They blurred her view of the king and his chief adviser as they walked from the library, their heads inclined in whispered conversation, leaving her alone to face a cruel truth.

Every precious ounce of joy she'd known the night before drained from her heart, like a spilled vial of perfume. She felt desolate, desperately alone. It was true, of course—Jacob hadn't told her he loved her. He had never promised they'd be together always, but he'd implied he had arrangements to make, things to do to secure their future. She'd assumed he meant a future for them together. But now that she considered the king's news, that Jacob planned to meet with a countess to discuss a union, and she reminded herself of his unwillingness to make any promise to her except that she and Cray would never want for money—everything, sadly, made a good deal more sense.

There was only one course of action left to her. She must leave Jacob's world and return to her own, regardless of the difficulties that would create for her family. But she couldn't bear to say goodbye to him or beg for his help to arrange her travel. No, she'd have to find her own way back home.

Jacob searched every room where books or collections of manuscripts might have been stored that would attract Allison. It wasn't until he returned to their suite a second time and asked after his wife's whereabouts that Gretchen told him her mistress had gone down into the town.

"By herself?" he asked. "On foot? She doesn't know her way around."

The girl shrugged. "I offered to go with her." She was preoccupied with changing Cray's diaper. Feeling devilish, the baby was kicking and wiggling, making it difficult for her secure the adhesive tabs over his plump tummy.

Jacob rested a palm on his son's chest and the child instantly quieted. It was as if the little boy understood that the owner of the wide, warm hand not only loved him but possessed more power than most men dreamed.

Gretchen finished changing the baby and sat him up on the padded table. "The princess said she had errands to run and wanted to do them on her own."

Jacob frowned. Errands? What could she have possibly needed that wasn't already in the castle? And it wasn't like Allison to leave Cray other than for necessary work time. Hadn't she told him just last night how much she was looking forward to taking the baby down to see the sights in town?

"I did suggest she go shopping," Gretchen admitted meekly, as if she sensed something might be wrong. "Perhaps she's gone to look for a dress for the ball?"

Jacob closed his eyes and cursed himself. Of course. The ball. A week before Christmas, one week from this very day, the palace hosted a grand ball open to all of Elbia's citizens and anyone else who considered themselves friend to the little country. Wealthy and poor, noble and common—thousands attended each year. And he hadn't even told her about it! So much had happened so quickly. So many things were on his mind. But that didn't excuse him. One of the maids must have mentioned it to Allison, and now she'd have to hustle around and find something suitable to wear.

"I should have called a dressmaker for her," he muttered. "Listen, Gretchen, if she returns, tell her to stay here and wait for me. I'm going to town to try and find her, but I'll stop back here in two hours if we don't meet up within that time."

Gretchen nodded, but seemed too busy playing with Cray to have absorbed much of his message. However, he didn't have the time to run through his instructions again.

Jacob set out on foot, fairly confident they'd cross paths. The town wasn't large; chances were good he'd find her. The entire country of Elbia covered only three square miles, and the town by the same name took up only a third of that.

As Jacob descended the narrow, winding streets, he stepped over mounds of snow, unmindful of his surroundings and thinking back to his earlier conversation with Thomas. He'd found Thomas in the library again, before speaking with Gretchen. His friend had looked startled when Jacob walked in on him. Resting on the reading table before him was an open manuscript so old its leather binding was peeling off in layers and the pages hung loose. Although Jacob had been in a hurry to leave when he realized Allison wasn't in the room, Thomas had insisted he read something he'd found in the ancient volume. The importance of the lines, written by hand in Latin, had only slowly sunk in. When he lifted his head, Jacob had smiled and Thomas had grinned back at him.

"So that's what you've been up to, old man. I've been doing a lot of reading myself lately. Guard this with your life," Jacob said. "We're going to need it."

"One other thing," Thomas said, before his boss could leave. Jacob raised an impatient brow. Thomas cleared his throat and scratched his beard nervously. "I have a confession to make, Sir. I've felt very guilty about something I've done."

Jacob stared at his friend. What was the man talking about? "Go on."

"It was I who leaked the information about Allison and the child to the London *Times*," Thomas said, then waited for a reaction.

"You?"

"Yes, Sir. You see, this woman, she was special. I could tell that you loved her but needed a nudge."

"A nudge," Jacob repeated in disbelief. "Seems more like a vicious shove to me."

"Yes, Sir, I suppose it was."

"And you're sorry?" Jacob asked.

Thomas looked at him for a moment, as if trying to determine the consequences of a wrong answer. "No, Sir, I'm not sorry. She is worth it. You love her."

The tension drained from Jacob's shoulders, and he smiled. "Yes, she is. She definitely is."

Jacob thought about that startling conversation as he walked through Elbia's shopping district, but slowly his attention focused entirely on finding Allison. Although the city was small, it was densely populated and packed with hundreds of shops, museums, restaurants and cafés. She could be anywhere.

He smiled as he walked, imagining his footsteps falling on hers, for she had likely come this same way. Every shop was decorated with touches of Christmas. Delicate old-world angels of glass or lace dangled in the windows of gift shops. The bakeries' windows were full of holiday tarts and breads and rolls—fruity *stollen,* iced sweet buns and *fougasses*—flat, crunchy biscuits sprinkled liberally with sugared aniseed, a treat borrowed from Monaco for the holidays.

Europeans didn't favor the miles of electric light bulbs used by Americans to decorate their shops and homes. Instead, they hung wreaths of oranges and cloves and evergreen, and boughs of holly and other greenery on their doors. The smell of exotic spices clung to the snow-crisped air as a fresh cloud of flakes descended on the town, which looked more like a medieval village at this time of year than at any other.

Jacob tried to think only happy thoughts as he searched for Allison, although a voice reminded him that it wasn't like her to disappear without leaving exact instructions for where she could be found, in case of an emergency. This Christmas will be wonderful! he told himself. This year he had a wife and son to share the joyful season.

People smiled and greeted him with waves and wishes of *Fröhliche Weihnachten.* Happy Christmas. Here, in his own country, he didn't need a bodyguard. His people had seen him tear about the streets of their town since he was a young boy, and no one thought anything of it if he chose to take a stroll now and then as an adult. Even the small press corps formally requested his permission before taking his photograph. To do otherwise in Elbia would have been considered bad manners.

Jacob searched the two streets that were most popular for their stylish dress salons. Then he turned down a wider avenue that ended at a seventeenth-century fountain ringed by small businesses and cafés, which were beginning to draw crowds as lunchtime approached. Allison was stepping through a red-painted door when he first saw her. Waving and calling out her name, he ran to catch up.

As soon as he reached her, though, he sensed an unusual

remoteness in her attitude. Her eyes slid away from his. She returned his light kiss without enthusiasm.

Jacob dropped his arm around her shoulders and started walking with her. He looked down. Her eyes were rimmed with pink, as if she'd been crying.

"What's wrong?" he asked.

"Nothing."

He glanced back over his shoulder at the door she'd come through. *Reisebüro*. Travel agency. The muscles in his neck and shoulders tightened.

"Are you planning a trip?" He paused, waiting for her answer. But she said nothing. "You won't have to wait long before we're able to go anywhere you like," he said quickly. "If you don't like Elbia, we can live part of the year in Italy...France...back in the United States." He laughed nervously. "I'm flexible, my sweet."

"It's no use, Jacob," she choked out, focusing on the cobbled surface of the street as she marched up the hill toward the castle. "This isn't going to work."

"What do you mean, it won't work? Aren't you happy at the palace? Everyone there already adores you!"

Allison's cheeks completely drained of color. "Not everyone."

He stopped walking, grabbed her by the shoulders and turned her to face him. "What do you mean?" he demanded. "Has someone said something to hurt you?"

"Frederik hates me."

"He's an old-fashioned pompous fool," Jacob bit off. "If he's offended you, I'll have a word with him and that will be the end of it. He has no right to—"

"I met your father," she said quietly, then let out a long breath as if it was a relief to have told him.

"When?" he asked, stiffly.

"A few hours ago. I walked into the library, intending to work, and they were there—he and Frederik."

Jacob's hands convulsed, gripping the heavy wool of her coat. "What did he say to you?"

She closed her eyes briefly, took a deep breath, then

looked up at him far too calmly. "The words aren't important. What matters is that he's right, Jacob."

"Right about *what?*" He shouted, ignoring passersby who obviously recognized him...and steered clear of their furious monarch-to-be.

"I'm...in the way," she said lamely. "Oh, no..." Tears trickled from beneath her pale lashes. "I wasn't going to do this. I'm sorry, I—"

Panic clogged his mind. "My father said that? He said you're in the way?"

"In more specific words, yes. And he's right, I am," she said firmly, dashing away the tears with the back of her hand. She looked up at him miserably. "We're pretending everything will work itself out, but it won't. What you really want is for me to be your mistress, so you can accept the throne from your father as is expected. But I won't... I can't..." She shook her head, unable to go on.

"I married you!" he roared. "Have you forgotten?"

She flinched and glanced down at her right shoulder. "You're beginning to hurt me, let go." He did. She sniffed and went on. "Jacob, the ball...the countess... Have you agreed to an engagement pending our divorce?"

He couldn't believe what he was hearing. What breed of lies had those two old codgers dumped on her? "No," he said firmly. "I've agreed to meet with the countess because I believe it would be incredibly poor manners to withdraw a proposal of marriage any other way but face-to-face."

The muscles in Allison's face contorted in a dozen different expressions before she found words. "You asked her to marry you?"

"No, Frederik made the offer, on my behalf...without my permission. Apparently, he was operating under my father's orders." He sighed.

"Breaking off an arrangement with her doesn't change anything else, Jacob."

"No," he admitted, "but I've been searching for something that will give me the power to do what I want with my life. Thomas beat me to it.... I think." He pulled her into his arms. "Everything rests on what happens the night of the Christmas Ball. I want you to promise me you won't run off with Cray until you see how things turn out."

"But, Jacob—" she began.

"Hush," he whispered, dropping a kiss on her lips. "You let me take care of the politics. It's what I do best." He grinned wickedly at her. "Well, I do have one other talent...."

Eleven

Allison's greatest fear was that Jacob's I'll-do-what-I-want-and-the-Devil-be-damned attitude would ruin them all. If he risked his monarchy to hold onto her and he lost the gamble, he'd be shunned by his people and exiled from his beloved country. Thomas had said as much, one day when she'd questioned him.

That was too great a price to pay. How could he then not resent her? After resentment would come hate. And with hate, love must die. She didn't think she could stand to lose Jacob that way. It would be better if she left with Cray while they still cherished each other, and live in the memory of what their love had been.

But she had promised Jacob she would stay through Christmas. And she would keep her pledge and love him in all the ways a woman could love a man, until the day came for them to part.

In the meantime, there was plenty to keep her busy. She helped supervise the holiday decorations for the palace. Candles were set in tiered gold-and-silver holders throughout every room. Men arrived with huge sacks full of fresh greenery, to be arranged around the candles and strung into endless garlands for draping along banisters and balconies. Jacob remembered the name of the seamstress who had fashioned most of his mother's clothing. She'd preferred the local woman to many of the European designers, who came and went as fads changed. He arranged for Helena to visit Allison, and plan a gown for the Christmas Ball. There wasn't a moment to spare, but the woman assured them she could finish the dress in time. Choices of fabric and style had to be made, then there were three fittings within the week before the gown was completed on the very day of the celebration.

When Helena unveiled her finished creation, Allison let out a gasp of pleasure and excitement. Not since her senior prom had she worn anything that might pass as formal wear. And the dress she'd worn that night had been purchased off the rack of a department store, at fifty percent off, because it was last year's style and three buttons were missing, which she had to replace to make it wearable.

But this...*this* dress had been made for her...only her, and it was less a garment than a piece of art. The butter-colored fabric shimmered and rustled softly around her as Helena pulled it over her head. The skirts poofed from her hips then fell in graceful folds to the floor. The bodice fit precisely, lifting her breasts and revealing a soft roundness above the neckline, which was detailed with hand-sewn seed pearls and iridescent crystal beads. The off-shoulder style emphasized her lovely neck and the shape of her shoulders. She felt like a true fairy-tale princess and nearly wept at the beauty of the moment as she stood in front of the full-length mirror in her and Jacob's suite.

"It is magnificent," she murmured, deeply moved by the care the seamstress had taken on her behalf. "I can't thank you enough for making this for me with so little warning."

"I'm honored," the woman said. "Anything you want for your wardrobe, you come to Helena. I will make it especially for you, Princess."

Princess.

The word returned to her at unexpected moments in the day as she hurried through the palace, worked in the library or sat at the long dining table sharing a meal with Jacob and Thomas, and sometimes even with the king himself, although he rarely spoke to her. Thomas called her Princess whenever they met. The maids smiled shyly and asked if they might do anything at all for "The Princess" or "Your Royal Highness." The titles began to feel less like formal labels than terms of endearment from the loving family of people around her, and she realized how terribly she would miss them all, miss her work here, which would be left undone, miss the beautiful art and furnishings that surrounded her. But most of all she would miss Jacob.

The thought of leaving him, though she knew it was what she must do, ripped her apart. Her stomach clenched and fought every bite of food. Her heart literally ached. But she held firm to her intention of returning to Connecticut immediately after Christmas, although she and Jacob never spoke of that sorrowful day.

"How has my boy been this morning?" she asked, walking into the nursery after Helena had wished her luck then left to prepare herself for the night's festivities.

Gretchen beamed at her. "Cray, he is so smart. He knows where his nose is, and his mouth, and his hair...don't you, Cray?" She hugged the little boy as he grinned and pointed to his nose, nearly missing it and poking himself in the eye.

Allison's heart melted. "Where did you learn that?" she asked him as he giggled and baby-talked at her.

"From me," Jacob said, behind her.

Allison spun around, her heart in her throat. Through most of the week, they'd only caught glimpses of each other. They had both been so busy.

"I taught him when I came to play with him," Jacob explained.

"In one morning?" she asked, surprised.

"Oh, no!" Gretchen laughed. "The prince is a very good

father. He comes every morning and every afternoon, while you work. He reads to Cray and watches him while I go to the kitchen to fetch our lunch and supper. Isn't that good?''

''Sehr gut,'' Allison said, trying to sound chipper. But she hurt so much. She'd been thinking of the loss of Jacob from her own life, but hadn't considered the equally devastating effect of separating father and son. Unable to cope with the dismal thought, she shut it out of her mind. "The gown is finished," she said quickly.

Jacob grinned at her as they walked out of the nursery, leaving Gretchen to play with Cray. "Can't wait to see you in it. Do I get a preview?"

Despite the shadow of sadness hovering over them, Allison couldn't resist his charm. She looped her arms around his neck and kissed him tenderly on the lips. "I don't think so," she sang the words playfully.

"Why not?"

"Because if I start to undress, you won't let me get as far as putting on the gown. Now will you?"

"I suppose not," he admitted, not looking particularly guilty. "I have another confession. I've cleared my calendar for the afternoon."

"Oh? And what do you have in mind, Your Royal Highness."

"Well, I thought if Gretchen took Cray for a walk, we might steal a few hours to ourselves, before we need to start getting ready for the ball."

"A few hours," she mused. "And you think we can find enough to do to fill two whole hours?"

He enfolded her in his long arms and kissed her heartily. "I *know* we can."

Allison ate a light supper of toast and vegetable broth in her suite before dressing that night. Tons of food would be served, she'd been assured by a frantic cook who had employed more than thirty prep cooks and servers to supplement the full-time staff for the occasion. But trays of hors d'oeuvres would not begin to circulate until after 9:00 p.m., and Allison feared she'd pass out from hunger long before then. She still hadn't adjusted to late continental dinners, and preferred her evening meals by 6:00 p.m.

She put Cray to bed before attempting to start dressing. The process took her two hours, partly because she discouraged any attempts by the maids to assist her. She wanted to be alone and prepare for the evening without a lot of fuss. Keeping busy had a quieting effect on her nerves. By the time Gretchen returned from her own dinner to sit with Cray for the evening, Allison was putting the final touches on her makeup.

"Oh, Your Royal Highness!" the girl cried. "I have never seen a more beautiful lady in this court. Never."

"What about the Contessa di Taranto?" Allison couldn't help but succumb to the urge to be just a little catty. She'd heard the woman's name whispered among the maids and realized this must be the woman who, even knowing Jacob was already wed, hoped to take him for herself.

Gretchen blushed and cast her eyes at the floor. "She was here for the ball last year, along with many others who tried to capture the prince's heart."

"And?"

"*Ach,* she is not so much. All...how do you call it? Silicone and bleach job?"

Allison laughed hysterically, and for a moment the fear went away. "You're awfully good for me, Gretchen."

Thomas had come for Jacob's clothes earlier in the afternoon. Jacob had told her he would dress in his office, since he still had a great deal to do to prepare for that night, and besides he didn't want to be in her way. She had a feeling his preparations had little to do with grooming or practicing small talk for his guests. He looked tense when she'd last seen him, as if he too might have doubts that he could pull off the coup he'd promised her and keep everything that was precious to him.

There was a lump in her throat the size of Connecticut when she answered a soft knock at her door at exactly 8:00 p.m. and found Jacob standing on the other side. Tears sprang to her eyes, but they were happy tears this time, as she surveyed his wide shoulders and tapered hips, clothed in a flawlessly tailored ebony tuxedo. A crimson sash sliced from one shoulder to the opposite hip. From his lapel hung a line of gold military and civic medals. His hair glistened a blue-black and his eyes were as bright as she'd ever seen them—with excitement or nerves, she couldn't tell.

"Why are you crying?" he asked, shaking his head at her and smiling warily.

"You're so beautiful," she exclaimed. "A man has no right to be so gorgeous."

He chuckled. "Flatterer." Then his glance drifted down from her face, lingering approvingly on the rest of her. "Dear Lord, you are dazzling, Alli. Every man in the room will be fighting for a chance to waltz with you."

"It's a good thing Thomas gave me a few lessons," she said. "I just hope I don't cost anyone their toes."

"You'll do fine." Jacob offered her his arm, and she slipped her hand through the crook, settling her white-gloved fingers on his sleeve. She felt regal. She was a real princess...and nothing this night would spoil the fantasy for her. She simply wouldn't allow it.

Jacob's dark gaze roamed the ballroom full of guests. There Alli was again, being whirled across the glistening parquet floor by a wealthy Viennese industrialist. She saw Jacob over her partner's shoulder and winked at him. She is magnificent, he thought, puffing out his chest with pride. No matter who asked her to dance, she accepted graciously. She'd charmed middle-aged accountants, dashing young dukes and elderly gardeners with equal ease. The women seemed to adore her as much as the men. Nearly every adult Elbian attended the ball this year, he estimated, along with notables from all over Europe. She held no person higher than the next, and every guest in the room seemed to return her love and respect.

He looked around again and saw what he'd most dreaded. His father and Frederik, sitting at one of the head tables on the dais, with the contessa and her parents. Frederik caught his eye and motioned to him to join them. The contessa flashed him a thousand-watt smile.

Jacob's stomach tightened, and he looked hastily around the room for Thomas. He had promised to be here by now, but Jacob hadn't seen him since they'd parted at his study. Where the hell was the man?

"Sorry I was late, Sir," a low voice said from just behind him.

Jacob spun about and grasped his old friend by the arm. "Thank God. I didn't want to have to start without you. You brought it?"

Thomas nodded solemnly, rubbing his bearded chin. "Yes, Sir." He looked as nervous as Jacob felt. "I just hope it will be enough."

"If it isn't," Jacob growled under his breath as he manufactured a smile for his father's guests, "we're all cooked."

"Yes, Sir," Thomas said. He cleared his throat. "Do you want Allison...I mean, the princess included in this discussion?"

"I think we'd better," Jacob agreed after a moment's hesitation. "I don't want her misunderstanding my meeting with the contessa. She's on the verge of fleeing for home as it is."

"I suppose so," Thomas said. "Can't say that I blame the poor girl. I'll fetch her, Sir."

Jacob sucked in a deep breath, tugged the sleeves of his jacket into place and started across the room. The orchestra played a swirling Viennese waltz. The music built into a dramatic crescendo that duplicated Jacob's emotions as he made his way between guests, offering them greetings of the season as he went. But his eyes were fixed on his father, as he concentrated on the words that must work magic in the next few minutes. Words that would justify and determine his future, and that of his family and his country.

The old man's face grew rigid with concern when his eyes met Jacob's across the room. Jacob understood what he must be thinking. If his son refused, tonight, to agree to take the contessa's hand in marriage, if he refused to accept his duty to the throne...there would be no heir. At Karl's late age, there was little chance of producing another prince, or even a princess. The leadership of the country would be contested by barons and dukes and minor nobility who could trace their families' lines back five hundred years to a time before the von Austerands ruled.

Jacob stopped at the table where his father's party sat and bowed stiffly. "Your Royal Highness...Sir Frederik." He turned slowly to the others. "Contessa, you look lovely as always this evening."

The woman lifted her chin, revealing an emerald the size of a hen's egg at her throat. It was a calculated message to him: *I am a woman of wealth and culture. I am what you need.*

He turned away and woodenly greeted her parents. From the corner of his eye, Jacob saw Thomas approaching, escorting Allison on his arm. He was whispering to her, patting her hand comfortingly. Jacob knew she must be terrified, not knowing what he was about to do. But she could be no more afraid than he.

Jacob held out his hand to her, and Allison took it, reluctantly allowing him to draw her to his side. Every nerve in her body felt charged with frantic electric pulses. She wanted to run from the ballroom, escape the condemning eyes of these people. She knew the king and his adviser hated her and would do whatever they could to remove her from Jacob's life. And of course the contessa and her family must view her as a nuisance, at best. The fact that the beautiful bejeweled woman was looking at her now with only tolerant curiosity, increased Allison's level of panic. The contessa appeared secure in her position as Jacob's next bride.

Allison's heart crumbled into tiny, insignificant, hurtful pieces. Some deal must have been struck while she'd been dancing. She steeled herself against the news. How she held her head high and continued to smile mechanically at the group, she had no idea.

"Now that we're all here," Jacob began, "I'll express my plans as briefly as possible."

Frederik shot up out of his chair with enough force to send a rocket into orbit. "Your Royal Highness, it would be best if we conferenced in private, if you have anything of importance to announce this evening."

"No," Jacob said firmly. "We've conferenced enough over the past twenty-nine years. Don't think I haven't appreciated your guidance. But now is the time for me to decide what must be done with the rest of my life."

"Jacob!" the king cautioned, fixing him with a furious glare. "Do not act rashly."

"I promise you, for the first time in my life I won't." He turned to Allison, who felt certain that at any moment she would drop to the floor in a dead faint. "My darling wife, I promised you I would find a way to keep you and I have."

The contessa gasped. Her parents started shouting in Italian at Frederik, who looked suddenly helpless. The king stared morosely at his son.

"Oh, no, Jacob!" Allison cried. "You can't turn your back on your people."

"I have no intention of doing that," he stated.

The group quieted as the orchestra fell silent. All eyes at the table focused intently on Jacob. An eternity seemed to pass, for Allison, while he settled his thoughts.

"I will assume the throne from my father on the first of January of this new year, as tradition demands. And I will do so with my wife, Allison Collins von Austerand at my side."

"But that is impossible!" the king bellowed.

Guests nearest to the table stared, then began to move away from the dais. Whispers traveled through the grand ballroom, as word of the royal family's discord spread. Someone suggested the orchestra play a loud and fast polka.

"No," Jacob said calmly, "it isn't impossible at all." He turned to Thomas and held out a hand to take a frayed volume. "This is a journal, kept by the Lord Chancellor of Elbia from 1535 to 1551. It records all of the legal decrees of the court during those years. As you know, Father, there are two ways of establishing a law—through writing, as in a constitution, or through precedent. If a practice has been allowed as legal in the past, it can be relied upon as legal in the present."

Allison clutched Jacob's arm. She wasn't sure where he was headed, but something told her there was suddenly hope for them.

"That is true," Frederik agreed, "but I don't see how this—"

"Listen to me!" Jacob interrupted, and his voice carried a level of annoyance that immediately silenced his father's adviser. "This journal—" he raised it toward the group and their eyes followed it "—this book of law and courtly procedure establishes a precedent in the court of Henrik von Austerand, the third of our line to hold the throne of Elbia. He took a wife, from among his kitchen staff."

A collective horrified gasp rose from the table, but Allison's heart soared. Now she knew what her handsome husband was up to.

"Henrik chose a wife from among the common people, but before he formally took her in marriage he set the matter before the populace."

"There was a plebeian vote," Thomas explained, taking the book from Jacob and opening it to a marked section. He laid it on the table before the king, who pushed the book aside with disgust. Frederik snatched it up and began reading, his lips moving rapidly as he translated the Latin to himself. "The residents of Elbia knew the woman he'd chosen. She was a good woman, respected in the town although she was a servant by birth. In the two years she'd been Henrik's mistress and stood by the king through a terrible war, she had been kind to many and won their hearts." Thomas looked at Allison and she blushed and bit down on her lip, shaking her head in disbelief. The two men must have combed hundreds of volumes from every corner of the castle before finding the legal loophole they'd been seeking.

Jacob took up the story. "The king's subjects, both noble and common, approved of the young woman. And so, with no one to rival her right to be called queen, she became Henrik's wife for life and bore him three sons, the eldest of them taking the throne after his father."

Karl looked away from his son, focusing on the blur of dancers.

"But—" Frederik sputtered. "But that was a fluke...an aberration from tradition!"

"You might argue that point," Jacob said, squeezing Allison's hand.

She smiled up at him, wishing he'd let her in on his plan. Yet maybe he hadn't been as confident of the outcome as he appeared now. He probably had worried about getting her hopes up, only to disappoint her.

"Yes," Jacob continued, calmly, "a good lawyer might make a case against using Henrik's marriage as a precedent. He might convince the cabinet and parliament. But I warn you to tread carefully, Frederik. If you refute the legality of King Henrik's heirs, born of a common woman, then you have destroyed all claim the von Austerands hold on the throne since the sixteenth century."

"But that's preposterous!" Frederik shouted, slamming the book shut and shoving it angrily across the table.

"Silence!" a voice commanded.

Everyone turned to the king.

Karl sighed deeply and lifted his eyes to his son. "You are correct. To deny you the right to a popular plebiscite would tear apart the fabric of our dynasty." He sank wearily into his chair. "You have won."

No one said a word, but after a moment Karl's glance drifted to Allison. "You must be a very special woman, my dear, to have caused so much trouble in my family. If the people approve of you, I hope you will stand by my son with grace and purpose. If the citizens of Elbia turn you down, I beg that you leave quickly so that we may put an end to this nonsense." He pushed out of his chair, then added in German, "God help us, either way."

The next days were so busy Allison barely had time to breathe. She and Jacob often skipped meals and they got very little sleep between meetings with civic groups, merchants and the working people of Elbia. The popular vote was scheduled for only thirty days after Christmas, which gave them very little time to meet with as many citizens as possible. Allison compared their campaigning on her behalf with running for the presidency in the United States.

But as tiring as their schedule was, she loved seeing new faces and talking with people about their concerns. She was good at sympathizing with the universal problems of supporting a family, obtaining affordable health care, and protecting their country for future generations. Most of the issues the citizens of Elbia wanted to discuss with her and Jacob were all too familiar to her. Hadn't she struggled to support Cray and herself? Hadn't she worried about affording a good doctor for her child when he was sick? And Elbia's survival in the modern world had become as important to her as her own country's continued existence.

"They know you are sincere when you offer advice," Jacob said, kissing her softly as they lay in bed after their most hectic week. "They will stand by you...stand by *us* when they go to the polls."

"I hope you're right," she said with a sigh. "I care so much for all of them. It would hurt if they didn't return the affection."

Jacob just smiled and held her close.

The day of the plebiscite arrived, and Allison couldn't eat a bite at breakfast she was so nervous. By noon, word reached the castle that a surprisingly high percentage of the populace had already voted, nearly unanimously, in favor of Allison becoming their queen when Jacob took the throne. Although the king and Frederik hadn't openly campaigned against her, Jacob told Allison that they subtly let it be known that the king was not entirely pleased with her as a wife for his son. However, as the hours passed and the votes were tabulated, very few were against her. By the time the polls closed, it was obvious that the people of Elbia stood firmly behind Prince Jacob and his bride.

When Jacob brought Allison the news while she was feeding Cray his dinner, she leaped up and squealed with delight. "Oh, Jacob—there's never been a woman luckier than I! I only hope I'll live up to their expectations, and yours." She threw her arms around his neck and held him tightly against her, thankful that she had won not only his heart, but the right to stand by his side for as long as they lived.

He laughed when he heard her give a joyful sniffle, loosened her grip enough to bend down and kiss her long and deeply, until her knees felt watery and pleasantly weak. "You have already exceeded mine," he murmured huskily, as he drew away a few inches. He observed her with an ardor and respect that made her heart soar. "I know you will bring my people great joy and pride over the years. I love you, Alli. I love our son. I love *us* as a family."

And later that night, while Cray slept sweetly in his crib, Allison lay in her husband's arms, her prince's arms...the arms that would be a king's only days from that moment—and they made love with a rich, enduring passion that was only right for a couple fated to rule the most beautiful country in the world.

Epilogue

Jacob stood alone on the balcony that overlooked the gardens. Two years had passed since the day he'd invoked his right to ask the approval or rejection of his subjects for the woman he loved and wanted to keep forever. Two years, and so much had happened since then.

As he stood on the balcony, dressed for another Christmas Ball, he watched his guests begin to gather outside the castle wall. Slowly they were let in through the gates, but they didn't immediately enter the palace, although the night was cold. Men, women and children gathered in the garden and looked up expectantly at the lighted balcony where the young king stood, alone.

"If you don't want to join me tonight, I'll understand," he said in a soft voice, not meant to carry beyond the room behind him.

"You might, but *they* won't," a silky voice whispered.

He turned and his heart swelled with pride as he drank in the loveliness of his queen. "You look exquisite, Alli," he murmured, pulling her out onto the balcony with him.

At the first sight of their young queen, the crowd went wild. She wore a gown of lush red velvet, trimmed with white fur at the cuffs and throat. A white rose from her husband was pinned above her left breast.

"Are you feeling strong enough?" he asked.

"Yes," she answered. "But I may limit my quota of waltzes tonight."

He smiled as he moved behind her and wrapped his arms around her body, holding her close to his chest. She waved to the crowd, and they cheered.

"How's the new baby?" a woman near the front called up to her.

"She's perfect!" Alli cried down. "She has the prince's eyes."

"Ahh!" the crowd gave a collective sigh.

"Is she sleeping?" Jacob asked.

Allison nodded, and looked up at him, joy sparkling in her sea blue eyes. She'd given birth just one week ago, and already she was up and managing the children and helping with the holiday preparations. "So is Cray. Gretchen is already here. Shall we go down to greet our guests?"

"Absolutely," he said.

It was a point of special gladness for him that his father would be with them that night. Although the old man had been gruff and sometimes outright nasty about accepting Alli as his lawful daughter-in-law, he had come around after about six months. As she'd charmed the people of Elbia, so she'd patiently won over Karl. He'd grown to love his daughter from America, and Jacob had come to understand the man better than he'd believed possible. A warmth had grown between father and son, with Alli's encouragement. She'd even coaxed Karl into trying a low-fat diet, and his health had improved.

Jacob stopped in the middle of their suite and turned Alli into his arms. "I love you," he said.

"I know." She gazed up at him with pure joy and stretched up on tiptoe to kiss him on the lips, then studied his expression. "What are you thinking?"

The words stuck in his throat. How could he say all that was in his heart? The strength of her love had carried them to this miraculous place in their lives. "Thank you," he choked out.

She scowled prettily at him. "For what, husband?"

"For everything," he said, thinking of his children, his father, his prospering country. "For everything, Alli."

* * * * *

SILHOUETTE® *Desire*®

15 YEARS OF GUARANTEED
GOOD READING!

Desire has always brought you satisfying novels that let you escape into a world of endless possibilities—with heroines who are in control of their lives and heroes who bring them passionate romance beyond their wildest dreams.

When you pick up a Silhouette Desire, you can be confident that you won't be disappointed. Desire always has six fresh and exciting titles every month by your favorite authors—**Diana Palmer, Ann Major, Dixie Browning, Lass Small and BJ James,** just to name a few. Watch for extraspecial stories by these and other authors in **October, November and December 1997** as we celebrate **Desire's 15th anniversary.**

Indulge yourself with three months of top authors and fabulous reading...we even have a fantastic promotion waiting for you!

Pick up a Silhouette Desire... it's what women want today.

Available at your favorite retail outlet.

Take 4 bestselling love stories FREE

Plus get a FREE surprise gift!

Special Limited-time Offer

Mail to Silhouette Reader Service™

3010 Walden Avenue
P.O. Box 1867
Buffalo, N.Y. 14240-1867

YES! Please send me 4 free Silhouette Desire® novels and my free surprise gift. Then send me 6 brand-new novels every month, which I will receive months before they appear in bookstores. Bill me at the low price of $2.90 each plus 25¢ delivery and applicable sales tax, if any.* That's the complete price and a savings of over 10% off the cover prices—quite a bargain! I understand that accepting the books and gift places me under no obligation ever to buy any books. I can always return a shipment and cancel at any time. Even if I never buy another book from Silhouette, the 4 free books and the surprise gift are mine to keep forever.

225 BPA A3UU

Name	(PLEASE PRINT)	
Address	Apt. No.	
City	State	Zip

This offer is limited to one order per household and not valid to present Silhouette Desire® subscribers. *Terms and prices are subject to change without notice.
Sales tax applicable in N.Y.

Desire Crystal Sweepstakes
Official Rules—No Purchase Necessary

To enter, complete an Official Entry Form or 3" x 5" card by hand printing the words "Desire Crystal Sweepstakes," your name and address thereon and mailing it to: in the U.S., Desire Crystal Sweepstakes, P.O. Box 9076, Buffalo, NY 14269-9076; in Canada, Desire Crystal Sweepstakes, P.O. Box 637, Fort Erie, Ontario L2A 5X3. Limit: one entry per envelope, one prize to an individual, family or organization. Entries must be sent via first-class mail and be received no later than 12/31/97. No responsibility is assumed for lost, late, misdirected or nondelivered mail.

Winners will be selected in random drawings (to be conducted no later than 1/31/98) from among all eligible entries received by D. L. Blair, Inc., an independent judging organization whose decisions are final. The prizes and their approximate values are: Grand Prize—a Mikasa Crystal Vase ($140 U.S.); 4 Second Prizes—a set of 4 Mikasa Crystal Champagne Flutes ($50 U.S. each set).

Sweepstakes offer is open only to residents of the U.S. (except Puerto Rico) and Canada who are 18 years of age or older, except employees and immediate family members of Harlequin Enterprises, Ltd., their affiliates, subsidiaries and all other agencies, entities and persons connected with the use, marketing or conduct of this sweepstakes. All applicable laws and regulations apply. Offer void wherever prohibited by law. Taxes and/or duties on prizes are the sole responsibility of the winners. Any litigation within the province of Quebec respecting the conduct and awarding of a prize in this sweepstakes may be submitted to the Régie des alcools, des courses et des jeux. All prizes will be awarded; winners will be notified by mail. No substitution for prizes is permitted. Odds of winning are dependent upon the number of eligible entries received.

Any prize or prize notification returned as undeliverable may result in the awarding of that prize to an alternative winner. By acceptance of their prize, winners consent to use of their names, photographs or likenesses for purposes of advertising, trade and promotion on behalf of Harlequin Enterprises, Ltd., without further compensation unless prohibited by law. In order to win a prize, residents of Canada will be required to correctly answer a time-limited, arithmetical skill-testing question administered by mail.

For a list of winners (available after January 31, 1998), send a separate stamped, self-addressed envelope to: Desire Crystal Sweepstakes 5309 Winners, P.O. Box 4200, Blair, NE 68009-4200, U.S.A.

Sweepstakes sponsored by Harlequin Enterprises Ltd., P.O. Box 9042, Buffalo, NY 14269-9042.

As seen on TV!
Free Gift Offer

With a Free Gift proof-of-purchase from any Silhouette® book,
you can receive a beautiful cubic zirconia pendant.

This gorgeous marquise-shaped stone is a genuine cubic
zirconia—accented by an 18" gold tone necklace.

(Approximate retail value $19.95)

Send for yours today...
compliments of 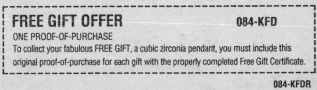 *Silhouette*®

To receive your free gift, a cubic zirconia pendant, send us one original proof-of-purchase, photocopies not accepted, from the back of any Silhouette Romance™, Silhouette Desire®, Silhouette Special Edition®, Silhouette Intimate Moments® or Silhouette Yours Truly™ title available at your favorite retail outlet, together with the Free Gift Certificate, plus a check or money order for $1.65 U.S./$2.15 CAN. (do not send cash) to cover postage and handling, payable to Silhouette Free Gift Offer. We will send you the specified gift. Allow 6 to 8 weeks for delivery. Offer good until December 31, 1997, or while quantities last. Offer valid in the U.S. and Canada only.

Free Gift Certificate

Name: _____

Address: _____

City: _____ State/Province: _____ Zip/Postal Code: _____

Mail this certificate, one proof-of-purchase and a check or money order for postage and handling to: SILHOUETTE FREE GIFT OFFER 1997. In the U.S.: 3010 Walden Avenue, P.O. Box 9077, Buffalo NY 14269-9077. In Canada: P.O. Box 613, Fort Erie, Ontario L2Z 5X3.

FREE GIFT OFFER   084-KFD
ONE PROOF-OF-PURCHASE
To collect your fabulous FREE GIFT, a cubic zirconia pendant, you must include this
original proof-of-purchase for each gift with the properly completed Free Gift Certificate.

084-KFDR